The Jackson Creek Road

The Jackson Creek Road

Essays and Short Fiction

RALPH BEER

ISBN-13: 9780997322118
ISBN-10: 099732211X
Library of Congress Control Number: 2016935729
Casey Peak Press, Livermore, CO

Cover photograph by Sheila Roberts

Also by Ralph Beer

The Blind Corral
In These Hills

Dedication

*This book is for my father, who was a blacksmith,
and my friend, Sam Curtis, who was a writer,
and my uncle, Ted Schuele, who is sawing lumber still.
Three of the best and so beautiful in the woods.*

*In memory of my mother, Ellen Davis Beer.
And her grandfather, Fred Bessette, who was
killed by a runaway team in the hills
above the Jackson Creek Road.*

Contents

Introduction

It seemed to begin right there, as soon as we crossed the cattleguard, where the Jackson Creek Road left the highway to Butte. It's where Dad always stopped, those long-ago winter afternoons, to put the tire chains on his 1940 Ford pickup. I would stand in the road and watch as he rolled onto his back under the truck to hook the inside links, then knelt and fastened the outside chains. All about us the snow lay jeweled in the late light, the cured grass that rose through it, tan and limber and still. By the time Dad brushed the snow from his mackinaw and unloaded my Flyer, I would be shaking in the cold and burning to be off.

Dad put my sled behind the truck and looped a length of cotton rope—tied at one end to the sled's center pivot—around the truck's trailer hitch ball, then back to where I sat with my feet on the Flyer's steering arms. He would hand me the rope and remind me to keep my feet up. "If you get in trouble," he'd say, "just let go."

The slack left the rope and the sled jerked forward and we swung off up the Jackson Creek Road, snow roostering from the rear tires, side-chains tapping a fender brace. We likely never left low gear, but gliding along eight inches above the ground, free to steer left or right as I chose, I might as well have had wings. My eyes watered and my tears froze at my temples and I laughed out loud with the thrill of speeding along so close to the ground. In memory I see us crossing the flat on the old Flaven Place, headed right into the low sun, the hills and pastures all about us as sweet and pure as life itself.

At Clark's Creek, Dad loaded my sled, and I climbed back into the cab where the heater whirred and sometimes produced warmth.

If the grade called Cutler Hill was drifted closed, he left the road to drive the wind-swept ridges that headed east. From there we could see the heavy snows turning pink on the peaks of the Elkhorn Range and my grandfather's land off south, where great heaps of granite stood above his fields like storybook ruins where giants once lived. Dad drove south following one bare ridge to another until we passed the timbered gallus frame of the abandoned Veracruz silver mine. Then we dropped into the sheltering pines and went on to the pole gate that marked the edge of the first Beer Homestead, where a cluster of log and batten buildings stood humped against the cold.

That would have been the winter of 1953-54, when I watched the clock in my first-grade classroom until Dad picked me up after he got off work. That he came to get me was an act of great generosity from a man who seemed to work all the time. Since he had to double back into Helena to fetch me, he could have saved himself half an hour of daylight by leaving me in town. But he took the time and made the effort, and because he did, I began to learn our country at the same time I learned to read.

Maybe it was his way of having some fun, after hammering yellow-hot steel for eight hours, and maybe he was trying to show me something he loved. But that's where it all began, the eagerness that burned in me all those years when I turned off the highway to the Jackson Creek Road, and the joy I found there, in the grasslands and timbered hills all around it, whenever I made my way home.

My family was there on Jackson Creek ninety years. The ranch was never much of a place, situated as it was in the granite and lime rock foothills on the eastern flank of the Divide. It was nine hundred steep acres of rocks and timber and bitterbrush that had only provided a living when the place was a dairy during the Depression. And it had been a hard go then. It was the kind of place that wore people out or made them sad in ways they couldn't explain. It was the kind of place—and there were lots of them in Montana then—where someone in the family always had a job in town or on the railroad or in a mine, to help pay the bills. My father and his father died there, and I almost did. It was the kind of place, you see, that would get hold of your heart and wrap itself around your soul, like tree roots around a stone, until you loved it like fire and would do damned near anything for it. Feeling like that can get a man in trouble, and a time came when I had to let it go and leave for good.

Most of the pieces in this book were written between 1978 and 1998. After Maggie and I sold the ranch in 2000, I stopped writing for nine years. Much of what I wrote during those twenty years came from my home country, from something I saw or heard as a boy, or from my work, later, with my father and his father and our neighbors on the creek. From the dozens of story fragments that were told in my presence, I developed a fondness for people I would never know and for things they'd done twenty or thirty or forty years before I was born. That blend of place and country-people and stories well-told was at the quick of almost everything I wrote. Three exceptions are included in this collection: two pieces that come from my slavish devotion to motorcycles, and the other, a recollection of my friend James Crumley.

As I look back now, I can see that the people I knew during my life as a student and apprentice writer remain more important to me than anything I ever published. I'm thinking of the friends and teachers and lovers who welcomed me and helped me enter into communities centered around literature, humanism, and writing. I'm thinking of the people who helped me become a better man and more loyal friend than I otherwise would have been without them. The best of those good people include Sam and Sue Curtis; Mac and Elena Watson; Sheila Roberts Malone; and Lindy Miller, who, in Bozeman in 1970 and 1971, showed me how much fun people with education and wit and a wide view of the world could be. And I loved them for it.

In Missoula, during the late Seventies and early Eighties, I discovered people like Neil McMahon and Jim Crumley; Bill Kittredge and Annick Smith; Jim and Lois Welch; Ripley and Dick Hugo; Jim Rougle; Sheila Roberts, again; Rick and Carol De Marinis; Blue Ballou; Kim Zupan and Paul Zarzyski; Dave Thomas; Charlie Atkins; Big Fred Haefele and Caroline Patterson and Teresa Jordan. They showed me that it was not only all right but absolutely necessary to love good books and the people who wrote them, and they nurtured me during the years when I struggled, first with sentences, then short stories and essays, and finally a novel. These people gave me encouragement and confidence and friendship. And I loved them for it.

And, of course, there were young women, too, who sparked me with their attentions and soothed me with their mercies and kindness, and I think of them still with great fondness.

The small body of work I accumulated over twenty years seems something of an afterthought to the writing life I was so lucky to share with these people. It was my great good fortune that they somehow mixed and merged with the working men from Jackson Creek I've known, men like Laramie Wallace and Ted Schuele and my father and his father, to enrich my life—from seemingly opposite directions—to make it and what I've written possible.

It seems there were always stories in my life. In the light of the Aladdin lamp on the kitchen table at the ranch, I listened to my dad and his father, while they cooked big suppers of mule deer steaks and mashed spuds and scalding coffee, when they talked about teams of horses dead already forty years, when they told funny tales about people with interesting names like Uriel Reed and Lester Cotke, who did wild and absurdly human things. There were stories about fights and fence lines and terrible accidents that killed good men and maimed good women, and always there were stories about the work that had made the place—the wells dug by hand; the trees felled with two-man crosscut saws; the broncs ridden out in the big corral that centered the place; the haying that had been done with pitchforks and buck rakes and great hawser nets. Those stories came together into a patchwork world that was so much more alive and desirable to me than the life I knew in town, and I dreamed about those horses and those long-gone people until they became mine. For sixty years that world has always been my best world, my jewel.

In 1994, a new magazine called *Big Sky Journal*, hired me to write a column called "Ranch Life." From the first issue I felt miraculously freed of a seriousness that had sometimes hamstrung my earlier work. Jeff Wetmore and Allen Jones at the *Journal* gave me my head, and I discovered to my delight an amusing flip-side to the rural subjects I'd written about earlier with such earnestness. It was fun to just let 'er rip, to sometimes be playful, even absurdly human myself. So Jeff and Allen, I thank you for that.

I spent much of my life working with my hands to preserve a place and a sense of the people who once lived there, people who were my neighbors and kin. The road where I once rode my Flyer behind a 1940 Ford pickup is still there, but the countryside all around it has vanished under the houses and emporia and clutter of modern America. There are subdivisions and a motel, even a traffic circle; bars, stores, a fitness center. Everything but what was once best about the place: the open country, the silence, the handful of people rooted for generations in its meadows and swales.

The Jackson Creek Road is paved now, and all the old timers, except for my Aunt Violet and Uncle Ted, are gone. But I want to believe that something of that lost place and the people I once knew there, still lives in what I've written over the years. If that's true, then I've paid back some of what I owe, with maybe even a little interest.

Part I
Non-Fiction

Sanctuary

Maybe it's in my blood—some throwback to a time when England was a forest with hidden glens aplenty for nervous Celts fed up with Romans and Saxons and their pushy, plundering ways. Or maybe it came from those long-denied of my Momma's folks, our burnt-wood cousins off the prairies up north, where any stand of brush that could break the wind must have been cause for celebration. All I know for sure is that for most of my life I've been drawn or driven to the leafy shelter of a particular aspen grove, where, during dry spells, Jackson Creek seeks refuge from the world by simply diving underground.

For ninety years my father's people and I have taken deadwood from this brake, usually in October, after our cows have wallowed the timothy and nettles down, a time when the groundcover of wild rose and willow burns various wild reds. Perhaps that thinning and cleaning has helped the living trees thrive, those elders the girth of a man, whose white hides carry the chevroned scars of climbing bears.

With luck, some few aspen at the heart of the stand will have yet to turn, while the ground thereabouts lies coined with the very best kind of gold. Often as not, my bright saws wait, while I prowl or nap in thinning shade or review local news with whiskey jack, chipmunk, and wren.

Of those fine days we've each had and would love to live again, I've had some here. Say an October afternoon some years ago with my dad, when, in the radiance of that particular light, we would pause in our work to absorb the spatter of colors about us and be lifted by a sense that in this place some urgency in our blood had found its way home. Several times, when Dad was busy in another direction, I would stop and watch him work, a man nimble and quick and sure-footed, a man so well-balanced that he created a kind of beauty about himself when he was in the woods. I told myself then: Savor this. Remember it. I did and I have.

This place, too, was where I came following his death, when grief hot as a pitch-pine fire cut away at me and at what there was in me he'd left behind. That was the summer of '88, when Montana's forests burned and our creek dried backwards up its channel to retire underground for seven months. Mornings, I shoveled secret springs to uncover water for our cows; afternoons I sheltered in the deepest shade until moonrise, when Maggie fetched me home.

We were there just yesterday and plan to return the day after tomorrow. Maybe we'll saw a few sticks of aspen for the parlor stove, maybe we'll laze and lark about. Leaves will be on the move and magpies will flash down and pause to chat. And when they've gone, a stillness will gather us in, and give us time to pause.

Like you, we sometimes crave nothing so much as sanctuary in a place that remains pure, a place made sacred by memory and grace, where we can let life settle, let the world come to rest. Maybe some nerve born in other thickets will spark to the surface like our water, which, although it has been hiding lately, still bubbles up downstream, as it always does, in wild-hay meadows where *Métis* sleep

Headwaters 1996

4

SILVER

In this dream a general dressed in buckskins blows smoke from his pistol barrel and with a cheesy grin drawls: "They're heeere."

Gunsmoke pours from the windows of rail cars into bison that stand a thousand deep, ten thousand deep, in ghostly multitudes where numbers have no meaning, where blood soaks dirt in such volume it stains aquifers a hundred miles off. The phantom railbed becomes a ribbon of blacktop where recreational vehicles carry open-pit miners and the performers of orthodontia with their orange hats and scoped rifles toward the forests of the West. At airfields amid the wheat, entrepreneurs deplane with Krieghoffs and good cheer intending to send #6 shot into our big sky. The black apertures of shotgun barrels slide by, eclipsing the sun, the moon, and all the stars.

That's it. Rather than continue to strangle my pillow, I roll out, kick the tomcat, and pull on my jeans. It's a couple hours before dawn on a moonless October morning a week before big game season. Margaret is off visiting her folks, and I know there will be no more sleep for the big guy. Hard cheese for Ralph, I guess, so I make coffee and pull an old Carhartt over my shoulders and take a steaming mug outside to the edge of a field to stand beneath all the stars there ever were or ever could be. Steers groan in the barn lot, and I can hear them belching cud in the stillness of this hour when the frost has settled and all but hunters sleep.

I can make out the darker shapes of corrals and barns and the outline of our bluffs rising against the Elkhorn Range to the east, and I am carried away by the silence and the nightscents of cured grass and Dutch clover silaging along the creek to such mornings when I once carried a rifle in a hard leather scabbard and a lunch in a paper sack to the log barn below.

Can it be possible to stand beside the path that kid walked and see him again, his teeth clenched against the chill and a case of nerves, on his way to catch a horse whose very bones have by now returned to dust? For a moment such memory seems more like another dream, fancied up in the dark hours after midnight when the soul yearns and the mind turns back. But I can feel the kid's thumb on the barn-door latch, and, as the door swings out, hear his froggy voice call a name. "Come on, Silver," the kid says, smelling the horse before he hears the animal step around to face him from the greater dark within.

They found Silver when he was two or three days old, trying to nurse his dead momma. Undaunted by such a bad beginning, my grandma Mabel took the colt to the barn and bottle-fed him cow's milk until he could drink from a bucket. Where the kids went the colt went, one of the ragtag crew, and he was named, in all seriousness, I suppose, after the Lone Ranger's horse.

Silver went from pet to pest to knothead by the time he was old enough to break. My dad rode him out, and, after a couple wrecks and some wet saddle blankets, he started Silver on cows. Over the years snappier horses came and went, but Silver stuck, big, black, proud-cut, carrying the heavy neck and shoulders that betrayed the Percheron blood passed on from some forgotten stud. Lots of ranch horses were cross-bred like that, I'm told, well into the Forties. Good ones like Silver were tough, savvy, easy to be around.

Because Silver was a fixture on the place before I was born, he seemed as permanent to me as the mountains. I just assumed he'd always been there, and that he always would be. As if in another dream I can see myself sitting on his back, gripping his mane hair with both hands. We are in the yard at the north end of the log cabin, my granddad holding a sisal lead rope, while my father stands just to my right, ready to catch me if I topple off. When the horse steps forward it feels as if the very hills about us move beneath his shifting weight, yet the men are all smiles. I can almost hear their voices. At some time in the distant future I will feel this moment pass through me like a quick little pain, and I'll see it for what it was, a ceremony of connection and welcome which said: This is what we are, and you are one of us. It was a homely moment of great love, and at its absolute center, a horse.

We would leave the barn when I could see the steel bead on the end of the barrel through the fold-up peep sight on the rifle's tang. I'd slide the .25-35 into the scabbard that hung facing back under the right stirrup, and lead Silver by the halter rope (never the reins) up the meadow and across the creek and into the timber below the hay fields. When I'd got my blood going, I'd loop the lead around the horn of Amy Stevens' high-backed saddle and climb on and put Silver into a walk.

In the coming light we could see granite bluffs swelling from ridges that bordered the fields, and the islands of pine and stone that lay scattered among the summer's stubble. In swales that held moisture, dryland alfalfa had come back after haying, and its tender leaves, even turned by frost, were a great temptation to the mule deer thereabouts.

Always we hunted the edge of things, going along slow through quakies and new pine where we could see out into parks and fields, Silver taking his time down cow trails while I dodged limbs and watched for game. If we had no luck in the upper fields we would cut south to Bunchy Haab's summer pasture and hunt the big pine woods to the water tank at Saint Amour's, where we once startled a lone cow moose. Then, generally west, criss-crossing back and forth through scattered timber and a maze of graniteworks, passing among the waist-high pitch stumps left by the woodhawks, until we got to Eric Prim's homestead cabin, where, no matter what time it was, we stopped for lunch.

Prim's cabin was a log and board-and-batten affair built low into a grove of aspen. I'd put Silver in the shade, pull his bit and loosen the cinch, then take my sack lunch of pepperoni and biscuits and canned peaches to an arbor of chokecherry bushes at the edge of the cabin and laze about, a young fella free of town and school, with all of life ahead.

Prim's shack exists nowhere now except in memory, having been dozed some years ago. And already memory fails: Did the cabin have a plank floor? Didn't the door hang always halfway open on stiffened leather hinging straps?

In the afternoons we worked west, crossing and re-crossing the backbone ridges where bucks liked to bed up high in the rocks. Silver would get sleepy in the warmth of the day and plod along half awake and still be the first to see deer rising or moving off ghost-like in the trees. I can make no excuses for the kid, except that he was snoozing, too, or thinking about a red-haired girl named Sharon, who played the cornet.

Sometimes we just goofed off, exploring the ruins of the Liverpool Mine, or the big steam boiler at the Hope, or the woodcutters' trail to the top of Sheep Mountain, where the world seemed so remote that darned near any-thing was possible. But by mid-afternoon Silver would be getting tired, and we'd head back north and east toward home, where more than once my gran-dad came out on the stoop to watch us trail in.

We weren't too hard on the deer, old Silver and I, although we got a few. At the time I thought those rides were all about hunting, but what seeps back now is a sense of motion and a way of seeing. By the time I was fourteen I probably knew our piece of country as well as anyone. Within a couple years I fancied myself something of a cowboy and moved on to younger horses with a lot more sass. Silver spent his time with a buckskin mare or off by himself. One day when I came back from school, he just wasn't there anymore.

It feels odd, although maybe it's just the natural order of things, that in my middle years I've stopped shooting mule deer and don't ride much any more. Most mornings I hurt somewhere, but sometimes I can feel Silver's left shoul-der against mine, as if I'm turning the stirrup to mount; can feel that first step and his back and withers as he moves off with all certainty among the rocks. And once in a while, if I'm at the barn and it's dark, I catch just the faintest hint of the rich, burnt odor of horse.

Big Sky Journal 1997

Wind Upon the Waters

Pray hard to weather, that lone surviving god,
that in some sudden wisdom we surrender.

—Richard Hugo

It turned out to be one of those winters, the kind you heard about as a child from old folks who considered themselves survivors. The first heavy snows fell in early October. November blizzards, driven by killing arctic winds, buried pastures under drifts three feet deep and froze newborn fall calves to the ground even as they struggled to rise. Weeks of subzero temperatures brought ranch work to a halt and drove herds of mule deer from higher country to congregate among the cattle I fed each day. By Christmas even the elk had moved down from their mountains to paw the alfalfa fields two hundred yards from my door. Local supplies of hay, already low after two years of drought, began to disappear. Because they couldn't afford to buy more feed, ranchers began shipping cattle; some sold even their pregnant cows, next year's cash crop.

Mild days in January formed rippled sheets of deadly ice on north-facing slopes and in gulches, and I fed close to the barns to keep the cattle away from the worst of it. Weakened by weather, the deer stayed with my cattle, growing so used to me that I'd occasionally look up from my work in the cowbarn to see them peeking in the open Dutch doors. A pair of frail, eight-month-old fawns became so tame I could almost touch them.

One storm followed another during most of February, and the leaden months of overcast sky and stone-hard snow ran together in memory as a single gray test of endurance. I'd wintered years with deeper snow, longer cold spells, and, I think, worse wind, but for sheer relentlessness, this one seemed to stand above the rest, seemed harsher in a vague abrasive way that drove me indoors when I should have been working outside. Call it cabin fever or a high blue lonesome or just winter, once you begin to resent the weather in the mountains of Montana you've reached the point of leaving or losing touch with yourself. Tar-paper-shack homesteaders discovered this kind of loss out here by the score only seventy years ago, driven toward one form of despair or another by drought and distances, falling commodity prices and winter. O. E. Rolvaag called their sod-hut counterparts giants, and in ways that are hard to understand today they were, the ones who endured. Others, like my mother's father and my father's grandfather, walked away to windbreaks or barns with rifles and did not walk back. Capable and productive men, remembered for energy and heart, who broke in February; men beaten by nothing more than weather, who were very much on my mind early one morning at the end of that month as I stood at the south window in my cabin and watched fast-moving clouds shift through a spectrum of early colors, blue-gray to ocher along the horizon beneath fleets of wind-curled cirrus fired bright chrome orange. The first direct sunlight in a week lit timbered granite bluffs off south, the uppermost pines burning red, while lower, in the darkest greens of the forest, horned owls quieted after a long night of melancholy questions.

Within minutes the highest trees in the encircling bluffs began to stir. Even the dead-topped fir quivered, ancient trees, rooted so deep in rock they often die erect and for several generations of men continue to stand, rotting and blowing away piece by piece in the wind until only a column of heartwood remains above a heap of lichen-covered duff. It takes real wind to move the firs, but as I listened, all I could hear was the chuffing of my box stove, the teakettle gently boiling on its fender, and a family of magpies scolding my cat in the yard.

With a prairie jacket over my shoulders and a mug of coffee in one hand, I stepped outside and stood bareheaded to listen to it coming, playing through millions of acres of forest, stirring every needle, twig, and blade of grass, coming with the surge of an approaching river running full to its banks, a flood of air roiling off the Continental Divide and rushing north across the foothills toward the plains of Canada, the grandfather of Montana's winds, the Chinook.

Alder along the creek began to clatter, the frozen lilac bush beside my door trembled, and I could feel the first gusts in my hair, as warm and welcome as a lover's breath. By the time I'd finished my coffee, the temperature had risen fifteen degrees, and everything in sight was in motion: flutters of chickadees overhead, fine snow rising in plumes along the ridges, and finally, from the south eave of my cabin, bright drops of water, falling and caught by the wind to be driven like new tacks into the dry batten walls.

Two hours later, streams of water poured from my haybarn's high eaves, surrounding me—as if I worked between twin waterfalls—with an exuberant counterpoint of light and sound. The sky thickened once with scudding, bruise-colored clouds, then quickly cleared. In the twenty minutes it took to load the morning ration of hay, half an inch of hoarfrost formed on the granite cliffs above the barns, covering the frozen stone with furry rime. The temperature had risen forty degrees, and the initial effect of that sudden warmth was exhilarating, intoxicating. Calves raced through the feedyard with their tails straight in the air. A young Shorthorn bull pawed and bellowed atop a manure pile, and even the most matronly old cows tried some quick steps, trotting about as gingerly as dowagers in basketball shoes. And as I watched this favonian acceleration among my animals, seventeen mule deer emerged single-file from a cleft in the rocks; in the open, antlerless young bucks struck at each other with sharp front hooves; fawns milled, hanging back, then bouncing ahead as if propelled on springs; and two large does, the leaders, continued toward me, their great ears perked toward the load of sweet hay, their pace serene, as if they understood that an end to their long struggle with winter had come.

The wind blew that day and all night. By the second afternoon the temperature had steadied at fifty-six degrees, and I couldn't resist any longer. I left corral rails leaning on a sawbuck to peel another day, changed into a knee-high pair of milking boots, took my walking stick from the elk horns above my door, and splashed off into the wind through fifteen inches of slush toward the creek. South slopes had bared completely, revealing again pine needles, grass, and dark earth hidden for several months. The first dry gulch I forded carried a stream of water a yard wide that gained momentum and depth as it rushed over the frozen ground to disappear under four-foot drifts in the open meadows. The creek itself had become a torrent of foam running above its banks into thickets of wild rose and willow, threatening to wash out a stream crossing that had taken me long days of hand labor to build. As I watched brown water sluicing from the stone inlaid culverts, I remembered the old bridge that had once spanned the creek there, a bridge built by my grandfather, who had snaked great pitch logs across the water with teams of horses, then spiked heavy planks to the logs. No one had bothered to tell me when I was a little boy that our creek was too small to support trout, and I'd spent occasional summer afternoons fishing through the spaces between the planks. I remembered lying on my belly on the rough-cut boards and watching my line meander from sun-dappled water upstream into shaded holes beneath the bridge where several hundred tadpoles and one very handsome water snake lived. That I was drawn back again and again without a nibble had, of course, more to do with a fascination for the motion and sound of water than visions of rainbow or cutthroat taking my hook. And that enchanting force of water, I've since learned, is not only the delight of small boys, but a Western obsession, a matter of life and death for those who live downstream.

The Chinook causing my little flood had, in fact, been born over water, far out above the Pacific Ocean as an east-bound mass of moist warm air. As it moved inland across the coastal ranges, this air lost moisture; more precipitation fell on the western slopes of Montana's mountain ranges, causing the air to become warmer and drier on eastern slopes than at the same elevation to the west. High pressure to the south, centered as far away as Utah, then forced this warming air north and northeast in the characteristic pattern of Chinook flow. While known best for their springtime assaults on snow, Chinooks do occur year-round; midsummer Chinooks are common in Montana, and during drought years have a devastating effect on already dry land and crops.

Related winds are found around the world where similar conditions exist. Cousins of the Chinook include the famous *Foehn* winds of central Europe and the *Bora* in the Denaric Alps of Yugoslavia, where, in the village of Split, ropes are fastened along sidewalks as handrails for pedestrians caught in the open when the *Bora* comes through town at a hundred miles per hour.[1]

Usually less dramatic than the *Bora*, Chinooks in Montana have nonetheless caused such wild and sudden increases in temperature that numerical records seem to pale in the imagination: eighty degrees in a few hours near Kipp, Montana, melting thirty inches of snow in half a day; a rise in temperature of forty-three degrees in fifteen minutes at Havre, Montana; twenty-six degrees in forty-five seconds, again at Havre.[2] And, as far downwind as Spearfish, South Dakota, an increase in temperature from minus four degrees Fahrenheit to forty-five degrees in two minutes, recorded in January 1943.[3]

More interesting than their curious statistics is the way Chinooks demonstrate, in a region already known for extreme weather, the potential danger of sudden changes in long-term weather patterns and climate. By climate I mean regional weather (annual rainfall, mean temperature, length of growing season, number of days of frost, etc.) averaged over a period of years; by sudden I mean within a century or less. Chinooks, like droughts and severe winters, suggest harsh consequences of even minute alterations in weather patterns, not only for dryland operations in Montana (which have always been marginal) but for our entire system of mechanized agriculture, one that now depends as much on vast quantities of fresh water—either diverted from rivers or pumped from the ground—as on oil. Ultimately, climate change would mean even bleaker consequences for large urban populations now almost totally dependent on distant factory-like farms and huge amounts of imported water.

The past year in central Montana has been a lesson in extremes. Last summer was a season dry beyond living memory, drier, according to records, than the worst of the thirties. The first six months were the driest of any year in the

---

1 *1. Jonathan Weiner,* Planet Earth *(New York: Bantam Books, 1986), p. 111.*

2 *Carolyn Cunningham, ed.,* Montana Weather *(1982), p. 115.*

3 *Weiner, 100.*

106 years the National Weather Service has kept records here, and this period was capped by a number of days of all-time-high temperatures. The sky in May and June, when the rains normally come, became a daily cloudless kiln. Antelope bitterbrush and sage wilted in the August-like heat; pine needles tanned on living trees; cheat grass turned not its usual dusty red but *white*. Alfalfa burned over at four inches in the fields. Range grasses blew away in ceaseless winds.

Allegorically at least, that drought and its attendant ceaseless winds seemed a warning as well as a reminder that our attitudes toward climate, water use, and abundant supplies of food may be taking us down a primrose path toward a desert. Like a Chinook we have, within the very brief time since settlement, used, wasted, or fouled much of our accessible water. Some rivers in the West have already become so overtaxed by irrigation and distant urban populations that after only a little more than a hundred years of our presence, more water is allocated than actually flows between the rivers' banks. The Colorado River, for example, is "120 percent committed. Eighty-five percent is used hard—so seriously diminished in quality and with severe salinity problems that using the entire flow is hardly imaginable."[4]

Our underground rivers, aquifers which took untold millennia to accumulate, are in serious trouble as well. The Ogallala Aquifer in the Midwest has been pumped so hard that grandiose schemes suggesting diversion of water from the upper Missouri River to "recharge" it have recently been seriously proposed. Much, if not most, of this water has been used for irrigation of crops during a very brief period in climate history that has been *optimal* for agriculture in North America. The final wave of homesteading in Montana took place during a wet decade (sixteen inches of annual rainfall in the wheat country) accompanied by the warmest weather in the past one thousand years. In fact, only five percent of the time during the last two million years have the earth's temperatures been as warm as this century's.[5]

How long, one wonders, will surplus food crops continue to be a burden on taxpayers in a future characterized by harsher winters, shorter growing seasons, and drier summers, when farmers will also face depleted water reserves?

---

4 *Ellen Ditzler,* High Country News, *Vol. 14, No. 25, p. 10.*
5 *Cunningham,* 11.

The point here may seem like old news: There is a finite amount of water in circulation on and around the Earth, most of it inaccessible or unfit for human use. We are rapidly increasing our demands on the amount of clean water at our disposal, often wasting it on a huge scale to carry sewage, to generate electricity, or—perhaps most dangerous of all—to continue irrigation of surplus crops during a period of nutritional affluence, spending that water as if there will be no tomorrow, while in the process, leaching and eroding irreplaceable topsoils, even turning the land in some places to salt.

A slight change in global temperature, *up or down,* will affect wind and rainfall patterns, length of regional growing seasons, amount of water in atmospheric circulation, and, ultimately, food production. Such changes have occurred, and very quickly, within the recent past; the cooling trend, for example, that plunged grain-growing Icelandic colonies on the west coast of Greenland into the permafrost of the Little Ice Age did so in less than three hundred years. Solar cycles recorded in bands of sedimentary rock nearly a billion years old in Australia suggest that a period of sunspot minimum is again due near the beginning of the twenty-first century, the possible beginning of another Little Ice Age.[6]

Sunspots are, of course, beyond our control, but the comforting old cliché that we like to talk about weather but don't do much about it is simply no longer true. Nearly five billion humans engaged in consuming, defecating, building, farming, traveling, warring, and dying have an immense if still immeasurable impact on environment, including climate. We are like a hot wind upon the waters, and by 2020 there will be eight billion of us, nearly doubling our influence, as well as our current demands for nutrition and drinkable water. Although the long-range effects of atmospheric dust, smoke, CO_2, and aerosol pollution are still being debated (some scientists project a warming or "greenhouse" effect, while others argue that a cooling trend may result from atmospheric clouding and sunspot activity), the likelihood of climate change is as certain as that the change, either warmer or cooler, will likely be accelerated by human activity and have serious negative consequences for future, more crowded, generations.

---

6 *Weiner,* 257.

The history of the settlement of North and South America is a legacy of man bent on altering the natural possibilities of the land he invades, changing it as quickly and totally as he can, often without first taking best advantage of—and thereby protecting to some degree—those native possibilities. Much of the Great Plains, including some of the finest grasslands in the world, has been put to the plow, turned under to raise grain used largely to fatten cattle that would almost certainly be healthier for consumers if raised on grass. Tropical rain forests in South America are being cleared at a rate of thirty acres a minute, twenty-four hours a day[7] to provide grazing land to raise cheap beef for export to hamburger franchises in the United States at a time when beef producers here have been bankrupted by an over-abundance of cattle. Misapplication of plow has led to dust in the north, of axe to less and less new oxygen produced in the great but shrinking forests of the south; together, these two tools exert extremely powerful influences not only on our present food economy, but, by eventually helping to alter climate, on the price we *will* pay for food in the coming decades, an expense which may not, finally, have much to do with money.

What shall we do when it appears the sky is falling? Cover our heads? What can anyone do about the forces of sun and wind and water and climate? Our first steps must surely rely less on technological advances than on attitude adjustments akin to those we made during the 1970s when the tap was temporarily closed on our until-then unlimited supply of cheap oil. We must stop believing that our recent spell of good weather (like 35-cents-per-gallon gasoline) is permanent, and that no matter what happens technology will provide solutions. Technology, certainly, will be helpful in perfecting better ways of recycling water, of developing more drought-resistant strains of crops, and so on. But the myth, that regardless of our abuses of soil and water and air, technology will somehow miraculously save us, is as dangerous as it is false. As farmer/essayist Wendell Berry points out, technological solutions invariably have consequences which lead to new environmental problems requiring a yet more advanced technology, which in turn creates vaster, more complex

---

7 *Weiner,* 332.1

ecological crises. A more expensive, un-natural, and less helpful cycle is hard to imagine.

The time to rid ourselves of a laconic acceptance of abundant clean water and plentiful cheap food is certainly while we still enjoy both. Although there is very little official planning currently being done regarding changing weather, public attitudes need to be altered to create new practices that work to our financial advantage as well as for the preservation of water resources, just as smaller cars and wiser driving habits gradually helped to modify the ever upward trend in gasoline prices and at the same time reduce auto emissions. Because Americans now pay such a small percentage of their earnings for food, and because the land and water upon which food production depends is being concentrated into fewer hands, bets for big profits are now being placed that food in the 1990s will be as lucrative as oil was in the '70s.

Common sense and self-restraint must be applied by large and small users of water alike. Highly leveraged irrigators in the West can cut in half the amount of water they pump from the ground to spray on fields this season by irrigating only when necessary to save a crop, and then by irrigating only at night. Crippling electricity bills would be cut in half while almost as much water could get back into the ground, since daytime evaporation rates of up to 90 percent would be avoided. If widely applied, this practice would conserve subsurface water reserves, send a message to increasingly profit-hungry utility companies, and decrease the amounts of coal and water wasted at generating plants. Soil leaching would be reduced; the land would remain in production, and farmers would almost certainly lose less money on this crop than on the one they soaked last year.

Residential water users in the arid Southwest should stop trying to grow lawns with water piped hundreds of miles from the Colorado River, and fashion-minded folks in water-poor Los Angeles should stop laving all those cars. The Dusty Look will be in soon enough. Trendsetters should let that freeway loam begin to build.

In the five weeks since this year's first Chinook, when I began writing this essay, the snow has gone completely and fields have again grown dusty. Measured snow-depth in nearby mountains is only 44 percent of normal for this date, and it appears that the drought of the past two years will continue this summer. If that proves to be the case, I will soon be out of the cow business; ranch liquidations will continue, as will the stress on wildlife and native foliage. Grain and livestock production will continue to decline, and the responsibility for and control of food production will continue to be concentrated in fewer and fewer hands. Well drillers will work double shifts deepening existing wells that have gone dry.

Sometimes less really *is* more, and quite often the best improvement is to make no improvements at all. During a Chinook, the meltwater roaring down my creek is lost to me forever. How much better, I've often thought, if the snow would melt a little at a time and soak into the ground. Barring that, why not take action myself? Drill a dozen deep wells, shoot them with dynamite to form underground caverns where water could collect, then pump that water onto my fields—an ever-tempting solution to drought in an already semi-arid country where visions of waist-high timothy dance mostly in the mind. Yet Chinooks, like droughts and hard winters, have been seasons in a healthy cycle that has belonged to this place long before my great-grandparents came with plow and mower, seasons I must accept and use if possible, even when they work against me, if this land is to continue to be productive for other generations. On this place, where water is as unpredictable as the future and nearly as precious as blood, I don't irrigate at all, and I still carry my water indoors in a bucket, one bucket at a time.

Antaeus 1986

Rolling Stock

There's an unreasonable warm lust at play in the West, an urge nearly as sudden and senseless as those which once drove us to Saturday night dancehalls and last-call love. I'm talking about the sordid craving most of us sometimes feel to buy a brand new, totally tricked-out pickup truck—one of those muscular chrome wraiths bearing fender legends like "XLT Lariat" or "Ram." They are *everywhere*, and they all seem to be driven by burly males with cavalry mustaches and black Stetsons who sport nylon lassos and flyrods in their rear window rifle racks. We know that most of these wranglers are consultants, lobbyists, or mining engineers, yet we are drawn to their trucks with a yearning that is both wistful and piggish.

Out in the farmlands and sagebrush breaks beyond the blacktop, however, a rusting fleet of unlicensed and fading beauties pulls dust across the fields and down the backroads, toting fence posts and saddles, salt blocks and canvas dams, sick calves, cold beer, all manner of tools, and kids. These are the trucks of real steel and slack suspension, as unwashed and as honored by the people who depend on them as were the horses they replaced. They rattle and they smoke and they're politically incorrect, and we love them with a love that is pure.

Beginning with the slim hotrod Fords built in 1940, Detroit managed to get it mostly right until the mid-seventies, when pickups started to look and ride like two-door automobiles, which, on our gumbo singlelanes, fell apart apace. But those plain Janes built in the 1950s and 1960s are still with us, gracing our ranches and small towns with an aesthetic appeal not unlike that of the stone ax. Of course they leak lots of oil, the brakes are known to grab, and the radios and heaters have mostly fallen silent. But in their grand simplicity, these honest old trucks have carburetion and ignition that even children and cowboys can understand.

For some of us they have been lifelong companions, and, if they end up on blocks in the boneyard, we mourn them as we mourn lost friends. More likely, though, we tow them under cottonwood trees, get out our sockets and hammers, and, in reveries of frayed wires and hard grease, repair what has failed while rekindling something of the past. Pulling a starter the other day, I was surprised to remember watching my grandad count a short stack of hundred-dollar bills onto a Ford dealer's counter one autumn afternoon. Just like that, cash for a new 1953 half-ton right there in the showroom, where its cream-colored enamel paint and white, bullet grill seemed almost luminous above the waxed tile floor.

Twenty years later I dropped most of my muster-out pay on a 1950 Ford three-quarter-ton, the Jack Palance of pickup trucks. I'd like to think I was even then trying to recapture some connection to a long ago afternoon of gleaming paint and wax, but in truth it was the best I could do with the cash I had. And for five hundred bucks, such a deal: The mighty flathead V-8 of yesteryear cackling through a new Cherrybomb muffler; the extra-heavy rear springs that make it seem you are always going downhill; the rounded front fenders *outside* the hood, where you can sit with your coffee to watch the sun rise over fields where you will spend the day. Oh, and the little, bubble-like cab that comfortably seats two: a regular Montana yurt on wheels. Inside, behind the oversized steering wheel that just begs a suicide knob, lies an elegant, molded-steel dash with its yummy plastic speaker cover beside an array of gauges that work forever and a row of electrical switches which do not.

Some endearing drawbacks, though. The engineers at Ford forgot to address the idea of front suspension. Mine rides like an iron-wheeled ore wagon. The vacuum-driven wipers work best, if they work at all, when you take your foot off the gas, which, in rough country like ours, can make your life flash before you while climbing switchbacks during one of our summer gullywashers. The six-volt electrical system bleeds current year round, what with decaying cloth-covered wires, and a couple hundred copper connectors wearing a green patina of age. That little three-lid battery won't cut it below zero, so you might as well plan to walk home some nights from the lambing shed. *Plus*, the syncrosmash transmission is damned near impossible to downshift into second from third, so passengers, especially hired hands, darned near always take the liberty to inquire from beneath the oily siestaland of a lowered straw hat, "Drive around here a lot?"

Still, we learn to live with all this, and we smile in October, as, with the windows down, we partner-up with our special gal to head for the aspen in that most forward of gears.

Up in the mountains, though, the old two-wheel-drives quickly lost their charm. In snow and ice you didn't so much drive them and fly 'em. They went fearsome places, true, but always flat out in third, tire chains trenching the land. Not so good for the environment, plus it got old—going ballistic through the bitterbrush, until, inevitably, getting stuck right to the running boards.

Then those wonderful little flat-fendered, four-wheel-drive Willys trucks showed up. Powered by runty four and six-cylinder motors and prodigious gears, they crawled through the limber pine to the last windy ridge, where only the year before Dad's bull had to be snaked out in quarters. Narrow and short, the Jeeps we had on the place couldn't handle big payloads, but there was no more packing fence posts down limerock ravines on our backs in April or dragging fresh-cut rails a hundred knee-deep yards to the truck in December. The heaters never worked, though, so in our rigs there was always a dusty mound of old-timey coats to wrap around our feet and legs, much as our grandmas and grandads did in open wagons. And, with a top-end speed of around forty-five, with the lifters floating and a rod about to throw loose, it sure seemed like a long time to town if you were fifteen. Still, the Jeeps went where the elk and the work waited, and we blessed them for it.

Now if we were to talk in superlatives (and I *know* I'll get a ration of grief on this) probably the greatest ranch pickups ever built are the 1970 Chevrolet four-by-fours, trucks that if re-issued right now, exactly as originally built, would leave this year's models dusty on dealers' lots. Why, I'd swim a river of whiskey with my mouth closed just for the *chance* to own a new one.

Back in the spring of 1970, the folks bought two of them for eighty-five hundred dollars. They're both still at work here after hauling thousands of tons of everything from hay and grain, to stove wood and stone; after the abuse of all-night rips to New Mexico and British Columbia and Colorado in search of one kind of cowgirl or another; to just generally running every kind of errand imaginable on the place, seven days a week. But after thirty years of rough love, every little thing on them still works. Think of it. Eighty-five hundred dollars for two new trucks: the down payment on *one* new truck today.

To be fair, there's just too many good old trucks worth mentioning, each with its own quirks and follies, its own hood insignia of grief and faded glory, yet each one still running on what must be thought of as heart. Could be, too, that if we locked a hundred fellers with sunburned necks in a sale barn and bought 'em free coffee until they could nominate a Top Ten list, we'd end up feeding them supper, too, and come away with forty or fifty all-around contenders. So here's a glossary of those few that always seemed to make it to the tooter.

Any of those baby Fords following the company's adoption of hydraulic brakes up to and including the early Fifties' models.

The WWII-vintage Power Wagons by Dodge, the ugliest and toughest trucks ever built, especially favored by our high-altitude hillbilly kin and their broods for stump-pulling torque and that ungodly stout winch up front.

For just plain get-it-done work, the International, called Corn Binders by some, with those little round tail lights, set way up high, where they ought to be, about level with the top of a closed tail gate.

And how about those knuckle-dragging 1964 and 1965 Fords, all jacked up on "weapons carrier" wheels and such for even greater get-go. And for going to town Saturday night, or leaving town in a hurry for good, you'll want to shed that 1964 El Camino and keep her waxed. With a 454 stuffed under the hood, this little bunny not only whittles those miles to a nub but makes you feel like a cowboy again.

There's no end to a list like this, as any time spent in country bars talking trucks quickly makes clear. But even if the Chinook force of our reckless youth has run its course and our dancehall days are pretty much done, we are nonetheless still fools for pickup trucks. And, you know, no matter how much we might love those old buddies parked behind the tractor shed, we are all just secretly itching for an unforeseen windfall, maybe some winning numbers, *anything*, so that we, too, can lick our thumbs and count out those hundred-dollar bills onto a dealer's counter, and just once get to drive a new one off a dealer's lot.

Big Sky Journal 1994

THE OTHER JAMES CRUMLEY

When I finally caught up with Abraham Trahaerne,
he was drinking beer with an alcoholic bulldog
named Fireball Roberts in a ramshackle joint
just outside of Sonoma, California, drinking the
heart right out of a fine spring afternoon.

—JAMES CRUMLEY

THE LAST GOOD KISS

I was somewhat timidly holding a can of Rainier Beer at my first faculty/
graduate-student/local writers' bash in Missoula, Montana, the first time
I saw him. It was the fall of 1978, at Lee Bassett's house, and there, standing
above Dick Hugo—who was seated at the dining room table—was this rugged
piece of work who looked like a cat skinner or tool-pusher off a Wyoming drill
rig. The hard-looking gent made a sweeping gesture with his right hand and
shouted: "And then, she said I'd stolen the title—from *you!*"

Hugo went into a rapture of guffaws and the two old bulls roared with
laughter, apparently enjoying an inside joke. I glanced at Neil McMahon, who
was standing beside me there in the shadows, also somewhat timidly holding
his own can of Rainier. "Who the heck is that?" I said.

"That," said Neil, who was always in the know, "is James Crumley."

Jim Crumley will be remembered by lots of folks for his early detective novels and the epic scale of his excesses. He was, for almost forty years, a legendary figure in Missoula's bars, from The East Gate Liquor Store and Lounge and the poker tables in the Oxford Café in the '70s and '80s, to Charlie's and The Depot in more recent years. Hundreds, maybe thousands, of people can say they had a beer or toked a fatboy with Jim at one time or another. And it is true that Crumley knew and enjoyed an astonishing mix of people, from Missoula street characters to lovely graduate students recently disembarked from Smith; from part-time carpenters and guys who worked for slim wages in the woods, to a mob of graduate students and writers and artists from all over the country.

Oh, yes, we thought we knew him during those Missoula days in the Eighties, back when a bunch of us spent our time typing away, groping toward a future when we'd be writers and much in demand. *The Last Good Kiss* was out, and Jim was our bar-room celebrity, our dope-smoking bad boy, our ex-Texan who wrote about people dealing with failed lives and hopeless yearnings right there in Montana, in the manly, crack-on prose that made him famous. Jim had a string of broken marriages, a list of teaching jobs that didn't last, a bird dog named Bean, and his daddy's Winchester Model 94, which he would pawn and redeem and pawn again, as his fortunes rose and fell. He was grand company and bear-trap smart without ever seeming especially learned or literary. He had some bad habits and a good heart, and we loved him for both.

Jim died four years ago. Since then his old pals and former loves have taken their turns remembering him in print and on various web sites. Although we knew he'd wrecked his health, and that death was coming, his passing left some of us wounded, nonetheless. The old lion was gone, and that took some getting used to.

In the late 1970s and early '80s, when I lucked into some good times with Jim, he carried himself like an out-of-work-logger, yet he sported a quick mind and great laugh. In other words, the sort of man you'd notice right off in a roomful of people. He was usually the last man on his feet at the parties Missoula writers threw for themselves back then, and he was about the best company you could find for cross-country road trips. But to say he was well-known and widely-liked falls way short of the truth, because so many of us just flat-out loved him and his books with all our hearts.

There was more to Jim Crumley than most folks saw, at least at first. It took a while before he'd let people in. I was fortunate enough to spend time with Crumley outside the usual Missoula writers' scene, which could get cheesy and inbred. We once drove from Montana to New York City together to attend to bookish affairs that involved agents and editors and going to lunch. Jim and I cut wood at Annick Smith's place near Potomac, and hunted mule deer at my dad's ranch, where Jim used his father's old lever-action to kill a couple nice bucks. The summer I spent in Missoula working on a novel, we'd get together in the afternoons and drive the backroads, smoking a little of this and that, sipping cold beers and talking. We didn't talk much about books or writing. We spoke instead of things that mattered, like motorcycles and women and the places we loved.

Sure, the public Crumley shared enough vices with his detective heroes, C. W. Sughrue and Milo Milodragovich, that some people had trouble seeing where the man ended and his characters began. Jim's detectives were tough guys, yet during his years in Missoula, and on the trail of his many travels, Crumley would sometimes open, like the blossom in a prickly pear cactus, to reveal a sensitivity and child-like sweetness that had been there all along, hidden among the thorns. Although in later years he could seem remote and self-indulgent, he was among the kindest and most generous men I've known.

So I understand why, when I think about Jim Crumley, I think of him always as a man alive in stories about him, stories in which he was a participant, not an author. I can't begin to think about Jim as a literary figure or as someone I could reveal by talking about his books. I understand him best, I know, when I close my eyes and see him in motion, doing something gentle or earnest, unruly or funny, some darned thing his friends would remember and retell years later with gusto. Here, then, are three such Crumley stories:

In the spring of 1980, Jim and I decided to drop a few pounds of beer flab. Because we hated to suffer alone, we'd meet up at the Van Buren Street bridge and run together along the grade where the Milwaukee Road's rails had once headed east out of town. All right, we didn't exactly run. Like a team of draft horses who'd spent all winter in the barn, we lumbered along, coughing up years of cigarette smoke and hoping our morning would not prove a final humiliation. Crumley, though, was tough and surprisingly steady, a two-hundred-and-forty-pounder who chugged along as if powered by steam. Most days he'd outlast me, until I fell, gasping, into a walk after three miles or so. Then we'd turn and walk back, already talking cold beers and good smoke, while hoping we'd done ourselves no permanent harm.

One bright morning, when we'd finished our run and had walked back almost to the University of Montana, we noticed two young men, dressed in casual wear that seemed a tad preppy, coming toward us with a bulldog trotting at their heels. As we neared them, one of the lads recognized Jim and said, "You're James Crumley, aren't you?" And when Crumley nodded, the young man pointed to the bulldog. "Meet Fireball Roberts," he said.

Crumley couldn't have been more tickled if they'd given him a prize. He talked with them for a few of minutes, as the bulldog drooled and grinned, and it was easy to see, as I stood and watched, that Jim was every bit as pleased by the encounter as they were. He was like that. Never stand-offish, never condescending, but genuinely interested in the people he encountered. If you spent any time around Crumley back then, it was easy to forget that he was not only famous, but already had the beginnings of a cult following, too.

Jim Crumley will probably not be remembered as a fiduciary wizard. When he had money, he spent it, and he could be generous to a fault. More than once he sent friends airplane tickets so they could meet up with him for a few days of bad behavior. When his bank account dipped far enough into the red, he'd take a teaching job for a year or two. While at the University of Texas, El Paso, he sold the film rights for *The Last Good Kiss* and sent tickets so Carl Clatterbuck, Neil McMahon, and I could fly down to help him celebrate. After several days and nights of too much Texas-style fun, Crumley took us along to one of his fiction-writing classes. It was the first session of a new semester, a night class, the room packed. Jim decided to read a story rather than just send everyone home, as so often happens after the roll call on those first days of writing classes. His selection was an obscure tale called, "No-Class Chick," that he'd found, in of all places, *Easyriders* magazine, a glossy motorcycle rag dedicated to V-twin engines, tattoos, and photos of smiling girls holding up their tank tops in pure celebration of breasts.

"No Class Chick" started off as a pretty straightforward quest tale, written in the vernacular of motorheads who live in black T-shirts and ride only American-made motorcycles. The plot went like this: The story's main character wants to join a motorcycle "club" but is required—as part of his initiation—to carry one of the member's "chicks" on the back of his Harley from point A to point B, which happen to be a couple thousand miles apart. A minor inconvenience, sure, but certainly not too much to ask of any hard-tail Harley stomper, except that the young lady, who was to be the cargo, suffers a death that is as horribly funny as improbable, on the first day out on the road.

The story's hero isn't about to let something as minor as a corpse sidetrack him, so he lashes the poor girl's body in an upright riding position against the sissybar on his bike and continues the journey with the single-mindedness of a .45 caliber bullet. The body undergoes all manner of indignities and damage as the road unwinds, until, near the end of the trip, the poor lass's left arm becomes momentarily free in the high-speed slipstream of the bike's passage, and, flapping crazily, seems, at one point, to be signaling a U-turn into another dimension.

As politically incorrect and insensitive and awful as all this sounds, the classroom boiled with wave after wave of wild laughter. Forty or fifty people were braying and stamping their feet and pounding desks. Really. At some point I looked over at a middle-aged and very respectable-looking Mexican gent sitting next to me, who held onto himself, as if against possible damage, laughing and gasping for air while tears ran rivers down his handsome brown face. We noticed each other with surprise then reared back and howled like great apes. It wasn't until later that I discovered he was a federal judge there in El Paso.

The story *was* funny, yes. But in Crumley's voice it became a mad, convulsing celebration of the absurdity of human endeavor. And that was Jim

Crumley in 1984. The kind of man who could wind up a room full of strangers by letting them enjoy a wildly inappropriate story as they delighted in him and each other. There were no pretenses of discovering literature or the secrets of good writing that night. But I'll bet my Triumph that one or two people got so hooked on story-telling that evening, that they put in years of hard work and sacrifice, learning to write well themselves.

And so, one last such moment, one last little Crumley story: On a brilliant spring Sunday afternoon in 1981, Crumley and his lovely wife, Bronwyn, my lady friend, Blue Ballou, and I attended a "sneak preview" of John Boorman's *Excalibur*. At last, a big screen version of Thomas Malory's *Le Morte d' Arthur* with beautiful young actors reliving the ancient tale of a boy who pulls a sword from a stone and becomes king, a king who is betrayed by those closest to him, a king who is then mortally wounded in a final great battle fought between the forces of good and evil. We four sat up front, as captivated as children in the darkened theatre, while the story, accompanied by the music of Carl Orff and Richard Wagner, unfolded on the bright screen above us.

At the end, in a series of scenes, majestic in their bleakness, Arthur, who lies mortally wounded among the dead on a field of carnage, commands Perceval, his most faithful knight, to take the sword, Excalibur, and cast it into the sea. Perceval hurls the great sword out into the smoking waters as *Siegfried's Funeral March* builds toward a breaking point, then rides back, calling Arthur's name, only to find the king's body, moving out to sea through shafts of light, aboard the kind of square-rigged vessel Vikings would understand. And watching over Arthur's body, stands an honor guard of angelic heralds, clothed in white.

Maybe because that moment in the film and the music were so powerful, I glanced over at Crumley, who sat transfixed by this vision of a departing king carried into the light on the ascending force of Wagner's music. Jim sat there with a most beatific and rapt expression on his face as tears streamed down his cheeks to disappear in the short beard he wore in those days. And I understood, as I looked at him in the reflected light, that Crumley had seen something about kinship and fealty and faithfulness in those final scenes, something brave and noble and honorable that resided in him and probably always had. And I knew then, that in the hard man lived a gentle one with a big heart and a great soul, a man who believed in stories and in good sentences and in characters who come to life. A man who believed in good books and true companions and love. And I knew in that moment that he would be my friend always, and that he would be near the center of my life, forever.

Ron Scheer's blog, *Buddies in the Saddle* 2014

Whose Woods These Are

No matter how harsh the countryside in the background, what we see in those photographs of first Montana ranches is that almost everything, except the wagons resting on their tongues in the yards, has been fashioned from native wood. Squat cabins and log barns roofed with poles and dirt front corrals woven from brush or rails where gates hang slantwise from tough juniper posts. Nails are far between and square, and window glass some kind of miracle, yet those windy holdings look like they were made to stay. In these photographs, such structures seem as enduring as the sandstone bluffs and claybank breaks behind them, so it's odd that while populated with mounted horsemen and women in big aprons and earnest boys with fresh-killed game, we seldom see (from the Continental Divide east at any rate) someone posed before a woodpile, leaning on an axe. Branding irons and spurs and horseshoes speak to us, while the broadaxes and misery whips and buck saws that did the main work seem about as luminous as a pile of dirty socks. It's no big surprise, then, that the calf roper on Saturday afternoon gets a lot more attention than the same fella pulling a drawknife behind the swather shed at eight o'clock Monday morning.

With all the conveniences that followed the power lines to our places after World War II, our need for stove wood and such declined, and, as one generation followed another, the men most able with axe and maul and wedge took their skills with them to the grave. I try to resist an urge to lionize the gut-busting labor needed to turn trees into logs and lumber with hand tools. But in this age of hundred-cube Huskies and hydraulic log splitters I can think of no greater sign of defeat than the sight of a propane truck pulling into the yard on a place with a couple hundred acres of trees. That is the final surrender, right there, the admission that it's easier to rely on money than to haul your butt outside to crack a sweat and do something for yourself. Maybe it's not surprising, then, that the folks with propane tanks and sheds full of rusty tools always seem to be so concerned about money.

I want to believe that certain abilities track blood just as surely as the color of our eyes or the shape of our hands. I come from a family of woodcutters, and I note with interest mixed with pride that in the 1900 census my mom's grandfather, Fred Bassette, and his father-in-law, Grandpa Cox, both listed their occupations as "wood chopper." As far back as I can discover, each scruffy generation of my dad's people had at least one roustabout who sold stove wood to support kids or bad habits like whiskey and cows. Sometimes in my work I can almost feel them in my arms and hands, yet in the sober light of certain days it occurs to me that they were better men, in their torn overalls and broken shoes, than I will ever be.

It was my good luck to work in the woods, before the coming of chain-saws, with an old fella who was an artist with a double-bitted axe. He was a long-geared, limber outfit and ungodly quick, it seemed to me, as he cut rail-sized firs with three or four clean strokes from the right and one from the left, leaving perfect little V-shaped stumps. He was either-handed as a bobcat and as precise in his movements as a cellist, and he liked to work with a hand-rolled cigarette burning on his lip. His axes had almost certainly belonged to his father, those three-pounders embossed with the legend "Kelly Works" on one side, next to a slot for the axe's registration number. Imagine living in a world where hand tools had serial numbers the way rifles do today.

His overalls' chest pocket had a faint white circle bleached into the cloth around the outline of the whetstone he carried, and all his cutting tools, but especially his axes, were as sharp as cutlery. His Kellys had a sharp bit for limbing and knocking stobs and a scalpel-edged bit for peeling and blazing. When he worked a tree, he continually, and I suppose unconsciously, turned the axe so the edge matched the job. His finished rails and staves were as smooth as hickory hammer handles, and he would get right on me if mine weren't, too. "Limb 'em *close*," he'd say, then thumb the stone from his pocket to touch up his steel. He got his start in our woods with his old dad when they threw and snaked out the logs to build our cowbarn, and he grew into manhood selling stovewood in town by the wagonload to buy groceries. Such an amount of work in all weathers to provide the barest necessities would stagger good men today. He and I worked among the stumps his father left just as I now pass through the ones we made. One here, one over there. After four generations, there are trees enough to last four more.

Memory fails. In my childhood my father pointed to a pitch stump and told me how Fred Bessette was found resting against it as if in bloody sleep after his horses drug him to death beneath a load of cord wood. I can't locate it now, and I'm told by someone I respect that the stump would have been a mile or so to the west of the one Dad showed me. And this. Do I actually remember watching my dad and his father, each man braced on one knee as they worked their way through a yellow pine with a Humbolt saw, or have I conjured that memory from what I was told about how the work was done? If I close my eyes right now, I can see them flexed against the wooden handles of their saw and the kerosene can stoppered with a rag and the sweet sawdust, too, spilling from the blade's raker teeth. They are throwing trees for the lumber to build our shop, and I am there, with them.

We know with all certainty that fine things are endlessly lost. Thumb through the tools section of the 1902 Sears Roebuck Catalogue and consider the wealth being created in America before the age of gasoline. And gone with the tools, a whole world of skills. Who can square a log with a broadaxe today or swage the teeth in a Henry Disston crosscut saw? Still, we conjure essence from what we have. My Uncle Ted milled the siding for our house from native fir cut right there on his place, and most days, if I stop to listen, I can hear him and his son Walter at work in the woods just up the gulch. Margaret and I sell twenty cords of wood or so a year, and we make our own stove wood and rails as we thin our heavier stands. Sometimes it seems we're always piling slash or burning brush or splitting kindling for one of our half-dozen stoves. There's no money in it, and I suppose we could be off doing something else. But the work takes us out of ourselves to better places, where stone and stump wood and the swaying tops of second growth are as loved as the faces of our best friends.

Big Sky Journal 1998

Our Best Dreams

Wind-driven snow weathervaned cattle in my calving lot as large-animal veterinarian Les Pannetier walked to the polled Hereford bull clamped in my squeeze chute. In the wind, which chilled me through my coveralls, Pannetier pulled off his coat and rolled his shirt sleeves to the elbow; he dipped his hands in soapy water and ran his fingers along the bull's swollen jaw. Concentrating on the softball-sized knots beneath the hide, he lanced and washed each one clean. "Lump jaw," he said. "Well along at that." And he seemed a bit apologetic as he ran through my options: lengthy and expensive treatment, selling the bull as a canner at the local auction ring, or slaughtering him for home meat. At best, he said, treatment might stop the infection (actinomycosis) from progressing further, but the real damage had already been done. The jawbone had been honeycombed by the bacteria; the bull would be permanently disfigured, and was likely sterile, too, a result of fever accompanying the infection.

Pannetier pried open the animal's mouth and pulled the heavy tongue to one side. "Take a look here," he said. So I looked. Not real nice right before lunch. Pockets of infection were embedded in the decaying gums, and it was obvious at first glance that it wouldn't be long before my bull began to lose his teeth. As I stared into that gullet, I saw how I'd be losing more than just an expensive animal. He was to have been the key to upgrading the grass-fed range stock my father and I raise here in central Montana. He'd been a gamble and a sacrifice, and, gentled by good treatment, he'd become a 1,500-pound buddy. A registered Hilger bull, he couldn't be replaced: the Hilger family ranch, where his line had been developed, went under last year, the old folks bowing to the pressures of rural development and age.

"Handsome animal," Pannetier said. "But you can't do much with him like this. They'd just take him away from you at the auction in Butte."

"Then let's treat him," I said. "Give him the works, if it's that or the rifle."

Five weeks later, with the infection now stopped, the bull began to lose his teeth. Rather than watch him starve, I butchered him. The dream dressed out to ten boxes of hamburger. Bull meat: hard chewing and tough to swallow.

Most Americans have notions about farming, that tilling of soil and spring branding of calves, vague notions, nostalgic or romantic, perhaps, of hardy folks handling land and livestock in careful and considered ways; of energetic, weathered men and women; of people who live in the quiet dignity of fields and pastures, guided, perhaps, by personal ethics more elevated than those of, say, real estate salesmen. And we know from newspapers, magazines, and the evening news that these same people are right now facing any number of serious economic problems. Farmers are in debt: they owed just under $50 billion at the start of the 1970s, and now owe about $200 billion. Perhaps 40,000 farmers (there are roughly 650,000 full-time farmers in the country, and many more part-time ones) have debts equal to 70 percent or more of their assets. And those assets are shrinking: the value of farmland dropped 12 percent in the United States last year, and more than 20 percent on the Northern Plains. It was the steepest drop since 1933, in the middle of the Depression. The agricultural sector is slower to get into a recession, but also slower to come out of one—there has been little recovery on the farm. The worldwide recession of 1981 slashed demand for American products, and the strength of the dollar continues to make the cost of buying American too great for many countries.

Here in the semi-arid West, where farmers more often call themselves ranchers, we also face the special tests of a severe climate: the wind in most of Wyoming, the hard winters along the length of the Continental Divide, especially harsh in places like Winter Park and the Big Hole Valley. And there is the everlasting threat of drought on the eastern plains. Yet hundreds of small outfits somehow manage to stay in business, struggling along in debt or at least not making much money—in 1983, the average Montana farmer netted

$13,083, These are the family places, where two or more generations have owned and worked the same land, where small may be 400 or 4,000 acres, where jobs in town often support the ranch in lean years.

In Montana, most ranchers, along with raising cattle, do a certain amount of farming, growing grain and hay to feed the livestock in the winter. But just imagine farming this: a steep, windburned landscape littered with boulders the size of banks, where even during wet years the hills and fields burn brown in July, where the only source of water, other than deep wells, is an aspen-lined creek, so shallow in summer you're hard pressed to water a saddle horse. Call this Jackson Creek. Imagine it in the heart of Montana, where my father and I ranch, and where we farm a hundred acres of dry-land hay ground—land cleared one stump at a time by my grandfather and his father with two-man crosscut saws, dynamite, and teams of Percheron horses.

This has been cattle country for a hundred years, though in certain places terraced buffalo trails still contour the muscled hills. It's country that can wear you out and make you proud, make you exult in what is and what isn't there. Until recently, the only signs of man in vast stretches of this country were the grassed-over berms of backfurrows turned by long forgotten walking plows, and lonesome lilac bushes that bloom each spring, reminders of homesteads gone bust. In the 1980s, however, the name of the game has become change—rapid change which is accelerating beyond our wildest whiskey dreams. As if rocky soil, Dust Bowl summers, and killing frost weren't enough, we now see just beyond our wire boundary fences power lines, new roads, and modular homes on grasslands that had remained unchanged in most senses in recent geological time. And what is happening here is not an isolated, quirky accident; it exemplifies, rather, trends almost everywhere in the West today within a twenty- or thirty-mile radius of small cities—from the outskirts of Cheyenne and Jackson, Wyoming, to Montana's Paradise and Bitterroot valleys, to places like Idaho Falls and Coeur d'Alene.

It is happening just beyond the tree line on the far side of our creek—what Idaho farmer Burt Trueblood calls "the people problem." It goes like this: in the mid-1970s, young professionals with salaried jobs in town decided they would rather be young professionals with homes in the country. Toward this end, they borrowed heavily to build expensive houses on a short acre of land in one or another recently subdivided stand of pine. Contractors roaded the country to death and built, built, built, until today those secluded stands of pine look just like town. Thousands of acres of big-game habitat and pasture have been destroyed by people who, for the most part, consider themselves conservation-minded. Their conservation, however, seems most often focused on the extremes of pristine wilderness and ecological disasters, while ignoring the farmland in between.

Lately, local developers have come up with a new wrinkle: "Limerock Country Living." This living takes place on twenty-acre parcels of open white-rock ridge land with covenant restrictions so lax a school bus might qualify as a permanent dwelling. These parcels are for people who like a view, so first thing, after signing their thirty-year mortgage, they get a D-8 Caterpillar and cut a road up through the buffalo trails to the highest, driest point on their property. From there they can gaze down at the daily demolitions in the new open-pit mine off north . . . and make plans to chop their twenty acres into five-acre plots in order to avoid the sinister mathematics of high-interest, long-term loans.

The native bunchgrass, which sustained the buffalo and forty generations of cattle, is fenced into squares too small to support a goat year-round. Erosion begins with each new excavation. Knapweed, leafy spurge, and Dalmation toadflax get started in every patch of disturbed soil, and their seeds are spread by wheeled vehicles which drive everywhere in that open country that wheeled vehicles can drive. But as each twenty-acre parcel gets fenced or subdivided into smaller pieces, less and less space is left for new folks to roam. Their ATVs, Jeeps, and saddle horses soon stand idle as the horrors of Banvel, Tordon, Roundup, and 2,4-D are brought to bear on the weeds.

A landscape once capable of supporting a wide variety of wildlife, upland birds, and domestic stock begins—as soon as it is arbitrarily partitioned, without consideration for the lay of the land—to die. Country once full of life declines into a pastel-sided desert, glittering with the accumulated junk of humanity and patrolled by bands of feral dogs. A way of life requiring dry grass and space is squeezed out in favor of one requiring only on-ramps to town. Unlike the ranchers who preceded them, these countrified city work-ers produce little or nothing for themselves from the land they so arrogantly occupy. Instead, they turn their new homes in the country into castles of consumption. And what they consume, they bring from town—reversing the symbiotic farm/town relationship dating back probably to the invention of the plow.

Change, of course, is nothing new in America. Progress, and rural suspicion of it, have been constant themes in our history and literature. Early in the nineteenth century, when much of the continent still remained unexplored, James Fenimore Cooper had Natty Bumppo, the venerable trapper of the *Leatherstocking Tales*, declare in disgust:

> What the world of America is coming to, and where the machina-tions and inventions of its people are to have an end, the Lord, He only knows. I have seen, in my day, the chief who, in his time, had beheld the first Christian that placed his wicked foot in the region of York! How much has the beauty of the wilderness been deformed in two short lives!

The trapper, looking back toward better times, saw that from the very beginning of our history there had been no harmony—nor could there ever be—between untrammeled progress and the natural landscape.

Development, in the form of economic colonialism, first arrived in the West in the 1820s, as fur traders poled their way upriver from St. Louis to take what wealth they could from the natives and the land. The French boatman Jourdannais, in A. B. Guthrie's panoramic novel *The Big Sky*, was just such a man, out for a fast buck in raw materials that he intended to process and ship back to the growing towns and cities as cheaply as possible. This sort was followed by mine owners, timber cutters, and then utility consortiums—all seeing the land as a source of wealth, and not as the source of life itself. As the glory days of the fur trade dim in Guthrie's novel, a man named Peabody arrives from the East, itching to bring in more people, to settle the country. Unlike Jourdannais, Peabody looks not to what can be quickly taken, but to the future:

> When country which might support so many actually supports so few, then, by thunder, the inhabitants have not made good use of the natural possibilities....That failure surely is justification for invasion, peaceful if possible, forcible if necessary, by people who can and will capitalize on opportunity.

That sounds fine if you're an invader, not an invadee, and lots of folks out West have taken Peabody's advice over the years, including a coal company bearing his name that is currently razing eastern Montana—a company which insists that Montana's grassland is a price worth paying for neon light and video game arcades in distant towns. If you haven't had the opportunity to watch a GEM (Giant Earth Mover) in action, scooping sixty cubic yards of coal and sod at a bite, believe in this: it is a wondrous reaping of "natural possibilities." All that power, efficiency, and technology, all that alien iron brought to bear on one grassy spot, makes you tremble. And it makes you wonder, too, how much coal would have to be dug to generate the immense amount of energy required to build a machine of that size in the first place. How many months of digging? How many years?

Since World War II, trends in farming have progressed along much the same lines. In the 1940s, my grandfather traded the draft horses he and his father had depended on for thirty-five years for Ford tractors that turned out a mind-boggling twelve-drawbar horsepower. Progress. He could plow all day and not have to fuss with harnesses and hot horses when he came home in the dark. In the 1960s, we moved on to twenty-horsepower tractors, and then, in the 1980s, to forty-five-hp models. Peanuts. Up north, the wheat farmers are using four-wheel-drive brutes equipped with air conditioning and TV and with engines rated from 600 horsepower on up. This is good, we've been led to think; or, more accurately, to accept *without* thinking. And if big is good, then the bigger the better.

As the idea of bigger machines gained acceptance in the 1950s and 1960s, so did the notion of bigger farms. We came to believe that one man farming 400 acres with one tractor was more efficient, and thus better, than four men farming 100 acres apiece with smaller machines. Those who could and felt so compelled expanded, buying or leasing smaller, poorer farms and "modernizing" them into ever larger units. In the process, folks who were content with what they had came to be seen in the same light as the smaller machines with which they farmed: outmoded, inefficient, expendable. Insurance companies, entertainment conglomerates, petrochemical corporations, high-tech industries, even paper cup and candy companies bought ranches in the West and invested heavily (wrote off heavily, too) in their modernization, this at a time when rapidly rising land values made buying agricultural land increasingly more difficult for farmers and ranchers. Large farming became known as agribusiness, the business end often operated by executive non-farmers in distant cities. The family farmer, who lived where he worked, came to be seen as a picturesque anachronism, his antiquated way of life often seeming to stand in the way of progress.

During the 1950s and 1960s the myth that scientific advances and increased efficiency would enable America's farmers to feed the world really took hold. We were assured that advanced farming techniques would increase yields, that technological breakthroughs could perpetually improve harvests. In the 1970s, especially, as the threat of worldwide famine became clear, big farmers were encouraged to get bigger, to produce at maximum capacity by plowing down even their windbreaks and ditch banks (and replacing them with automated sprinkler systems, which operate not by gravity but on expensive electricity). Our government urged us down the path of maximum size, maximum specialization, maximum mechanization, and maximum production—to be achieved, however, with a minimum of farmers. Only now are voices beginning to be raised that all this maximizing is exhausting our topsoil, and that by century's end we may be witnessing shortages, not surpluses.

The great dream of American agriculture has been to make the desert bloom. And it has been done. Yet in the semi-arid West, where rapid population growth and water-hungry industries have greatly increased the demand for clean water, aquifers have begun to show signs of depletion. In *To Quench Our Thirst*, a study of the nation's growing water shortage, David A. Francko and Robert G. Wetzel write:

> Throughout the West, these varied and enormous demands for water have resulted in chronic water shortfall conditions unparalleled since the Dust Bowl days of the 1930s. In many areas of the region the situation has become so acute that choices between food production and energy development may have to be made.

Expansionism and production-oriented reliance on supermechanization, as well as an increasing dependence on expensive oil and electricity, have hurt farmers, except perhaps the very small operators who have clung to what they know will work over the long run. Good farming practices, including the spreading of manure and the rotation of crops, have been ignored by progressive-thinking agribusinessmen who have favored—thus increasing their dependence upon—expensive chemical fertilizers and sprinkler irrigation. Yet higher production often creates surplus, which in turn leads to lower prices. As with the GEM coal shovels, one wonders when, exactly, that point of diminishing returns is reached, when farmers must increase their debts and ruin their soil to produce more of that which is progressively worth less.

There are so many snags like this in our thinking these days, so many Catch-22s. As a people, we have accepted the routine condemnation of small farms for their smallness, yet we casually condone the subdivision of these places into even smaller "ranchettes." We fear the millions of unemployed, hungry, and homeless in our cities, yet do little to prevent the ranks of displaced farmers from adding to their numbers. Indeed, we seem to take a kind of patriotic pride in the knowledge that fewer of us can produce more, just as fewer of us with advanced weapons can kill more. We store great quantities of surplus food in warehouses and hide cheese in caves, yet the Physician Task Force on Hunger in America recently reported that hunger is at epidemic proportions. The five o'clock news shows us not only the starving multitudes in Africa but farm families in Iowa who subsist on potatoes rejected by local wholesalers *because they can't afford to buy food.* How could things have gotten so out of hand in our land of plenty that farmers have to worry about buying food, when it's farmers who *raise* the food?

We drown in statistics yet have little hope of finding the truth. But last fall, back at the ranch, my father and I took two truckloads of 600-pound feeder calves to market, calves which in 1972 went for more than ninety cents a live pound. Last September we got sixty to sixty-five cents and felt plenty lucky. During those twelve years, gasoline prices increased 300 percent and the price of machinery went up 250 percent or more. And of course everything else we bought, from boots to toothpaste, went up too.

If you work ten-hour days to lose money, sooner or later you'll sour on the notion that your rewards must be internal. The frustration at just trying to break even has taken on a new edge this past year. Montana now has a suicide hotline for people in agriculture: (406) 653-2492. It's not toll free. Last November, the Montana Department of Agriculture released a study showing that 45 percent of the state's farmers and ranchers believe they will go out of business in the next five years if current conditions persist. It's no wonder farmers are found hanging from the rafters in their barns.

Most small farmers don't want subsidized solutions or temporary bailouts; they want a price for their product that at least keeps pace with inflation, interest rates, and production costs. Farmers receive less than thirty cents of every dollar consumers spend for food—the remaining seventy cents being added for transportation, processing, packaging, marketing, and advertising. Together, these activities take only a fraction of the *time* required to produce the food in the first place.

One night last winter, while looking for a lame calf, I met my downstream neighbor, Laramie Wallace, on foot too, trying to find a cow he figured would calve that night. At a distance he looked like the scarecrow in *The Wizard of Oz*, his canvas jacket, jeans, and rubber boots a patchwork of home-sewn thrift. Despite the cold we stopped to chat over the top strand of our boundary fence, and when the talk turned to ranching he said, "Well, we're sure not in it for the money."

His remark has come to haunt me at odd times, like when I'm on my knees in the mud, up to one elbow inside a cow, trying to turn her calf. Although I might not tell Laramie this to his face, it sometimes seems we're in it because of dreams: the faithful, ongoing dreams that come with being the third or fourth or fifth generation to work the same piece of ground. For many of us there is a continuous myth-making process, a steady reinventing and renewal of ourselves which is generated and defined by one aspect of our rural lives more than by anything else: our love of place.

But the myths are wearing thin. The lonesome horseman, once the central image of Western myth, now lives in an Airstream out behind the swather shed, and he leaves, when his skills are no longer needed, not for the wilderness but for a job that often seems demeaning in town. "Successful" ranchers have evolved into country club trustees with winter homes in Arizona and pilot's licenses to help them keep track of the land and cattle they own.

At night, satellite television brings a stream of Western imagery so incompatible with our experience we wonder if we're ranching on the same planet. Yet the domestic power plays of *Dallas* are just plain more interesting than Grandpa's stories about the coming of the two-bottomed plow. But when Grandpa dies . . . when he's gone, so are most of his tales about how things were when the land was young—stories about men and horses, about feuds and friendships, about bloodletting and forgiveness, about brute strength and dumb courage; stories which became, somehow, part of our own lives—stories which, in pre-TV times, magically sustained us by fostering local legends, personal myths, and our ideas about how we, as Westerners, ought to act. And, without much thinking about it, we let these mythic notions lead us toward a commitment to stay on, to invest our loyalty and dreams in the places from which we grew, even as these places changed before our eyes like a conjurer's trick.

Last spring I attended the Montana Myths Project conference in Helena, our state capital. Perhaps three hundred people met at the Colonial Inn to explore the effects Western myths have had on our sense of ourselves. One of the speakers, a Crow Indian named Janine Pease-Windy Boy, described eloquently the savage process of dispossession that her people still face, emphasizing that today's contracts and agreements often seem to be no more binding than those signed in the 1870s. As she spoke, I remembered a story fragment I'd heard twenty-five or thirty years before. In the winter of 1909-10, my grandfather and his father witnessed on their weekly trips to town a large encampment of Indians on the outskirts of Helena. The Indians were kept under military guard for the duration of that winter, near the ground where the Colonial Inn now stands. These people were en route to reservations, having been forced from land they'd owned for centuries by the governmental processes homesteaders believed would safeguard *their* rights of private ownership. As I listened to Miss Pease-Windy Boy, I realized how many farmers and ranchers I know who feel certain—whether they will openly admit it or not—that they are facing the same dispossession that cost those Indians their land only a hundred years ago. "Invasion," as Peabody said, "peaceful if possible, forcible if necessary."

Since we do without many of the things most Americans take for granted—weekends off, new cars, up-to-date appliances—we have come to think of ourselves, by comparison, as poor. My father worked six days a week for thirty years before he bought his first new vehicle, which, fifteen years later, he uses every day and still refers to as his new truck. My old pickup, which I use almost every day, is thirty-five years old. Stories about the repossession of $100,000 tractors have become commonplace on the evening news, yet there has been little mention of the thousands of farm and ranch families who have for years sacrificed a standard of living most Americans would see as ordinary, even minimal. These families—who may have no indoor plumbing, central heating, or telephone, who work by lantern light in the barn because there is no electricity except at the house—run operations where earnings get plowed back into the place, where outbuildings may be in better repair than bedrooms. While often free of debts, these families are usually considered poor, their living conditions dismissed as backward, even embarrassing for youngsters who bring friends home to visit Mom and Pop on the farm.

Most embarrassing of all, perhaps, is that we still work with our hands. Hand labor in our culture has become associated with the most pejorative terms in our language: *wetback, redneck, nigger.* Farmers are perceived as inarticulate, unsophisticated, dull, and incapable of doing much else besides farming. Our society's emphasis on upward mobility, hypercleanliness, and ease serves to draw ever greater distinctions between farmers and middle- and upper-class Americans. The belief that handwork is undignified, dirty, even disgusting is reinforced by our schools, our television, and our advertising. To *like* working outdoors in all kinds of weather, often using tools invented centuries ago, seems downright simple-minded.

We find we have skills that are no longer valued by the vast majority of Americans. In spite of a mushrooming rural population, our sense of isolation grows. We see ourselves as a few, surrounded by many, with more on the way. We feel less secure, more vulnerable to violence from outside.

And here on Jackson Creek, we've come to worry not only that greedy outsiders will try to take control of our land, but that one of the adjoining ranches will sell, opening the floodgates for development right on the creek. We vacillate: one day we swear we'll tough it out, maybe circle up our balers and defend the old homestead with Grandma's pearl-handled Colt; a few days later, we speak seriously of selling to anybody with that kind of cash. Increasingly, we don't know how to act; we are surrounded by an alien culture which we see as oppressive and beyond our power to understand. And there will be no moving farther west. This is it.

When, finally, you're faced with the choice of continuing an operation which seems less viable every day or retiring young and financially secure, you realize that maybe it's a way of life you've been after all along, and not the good life. But when you admit that you're clinging to a doomed way of life, no matter what your reasons, a distance begins to grow between you and your past, between you and your land, between you and yourself. What ranching often comes down to today is a last chance of acting out what our best dreams have always demanded we ought to be.

Harper's Magazine 1985

[Author's note: In the thirty years since this essay first appeared in *Harper's Magazine*, the agri-economy has recovered from the dark years of the early 1980s. Crop prices improved slowly as did cattle prices. Land values in the early 21st century soared. More cropland was put back into production until land and commodity prices fell sharply in 2015 and continue to decline to this day, bringing the boom-and-bust pattern of American agriculture through another complete cycle.

In the Jackson Creek area of central Montana, rural subdivision continued at a rapid pace, with only minor slowdowns in recession years. Two of the three ranches on the creek have been sold. Half of one place has been subdivided. My wife and I sold the Beer Ranch in 2000. The Schuele Ranch alone continues to raise cattle and mill lumber.]

In Spite of Distance
The New Literature of Montana

A television advertisement offers, as part of Montana's upcoming Centennial celebration, a deed to one square inch of Montana and the pitch, "Own a piece of the last of what's best in America." The offer, of course, is pure Chamber of Commerce boosterism taking subdivision to its final extreme. But I'm intrigued by the slogan. I want to believe it even if I'm a little unclear about what it means exactly, an ambivalence most of us share about living in this singular place right now. Admit it, it's hard to name just what, in the vast and radical geographic, economic, and ethnic differences of Montana, gets its hooks into us, gives us an identity and source of pride, even helps create a unique and prolific outpouring of literature all its own. Yet always we go back, when attempting to name this itch, to place or a sense of place that may not always be connected to any certain spot on the map.

Because Montana is so dissimilar from border to border and from county to county, there must be other reasons for our shared sense of identity and literature besides lists of favorite places. And the foremost of these reasons is, I think, an unconscious but still active sense of the frontier—a feeling subtle yet suggestive as a half-remembered dream—that is a response to an accumulation of uniquely American mythology, a brief and recent history, powerful visual remnants of that past, and, most of all, a dramatic landscape. We know, even if we never go there, that the great Beartooth Range rises only a few hours to the east, that only a few miles west the rugged beauty of the Rocky Mountain Front meets the plains still frequented by grizzlies. Rising like sets of magical backdrops, Montana's mountains bear physical witness that we live in a largely unsettled, harsh, and fragile land in the foreground of even wilder, less hospitable distances. And while thousands of satellite dishes aim southward above these mountains, the overpowering presence of distance and the ever-present threat of isolation is for many as real today as for frontier farmers Richard Hugo remembered with the lines:

Even wind must work when land gets old. The
rotting wagon tongue makes fun of girls who
begged to go to town. Broken brakerods dangle
in the dirt. Alternatives were madness or a
calloused moon.

But to go back to what, for white Montanans at least, is both beginning to Montana history and Montana literature, we must begin with Lewis and Clark, who wrote what is largely a record of their sense of wonder at this place. Perhaps in no other document of the early West is the power of place so overwhelming. When Lewis and Clark set out in 1804, American attitudes were changing; Jefferson's vision of agrarian pastoralism was spreading before the plows of yeoman farmers in the East, and married to this vision of pastoralism was the enlightened notion that wilderness was not a dark, unknown place of evil as the Calvinists had held, but a garden, filled with life-giving potential for the nurturing of countless generations of husbandmen. Of course Mr. Jefferson had no idea that the West was largely made up of places like the Sand Hills of Nebraska, the Staked Plains of Texas, the Alkali Flats of Wyoming, or the Bitterroot Mountains of Montana and Idaho, and this oversight brought, just as surely as the Homestead Act and railroads, generations of grief to thousands of sodbusters who shared his dream.

As Lewis and Clark moved upriver, their early journal entries reflect both Jefferson's idea of wilderness as Edenic and their own simple joy to be moving through such country. They were, those first months upon the river, as if at play in the fields of the Lord. They had entered the Garden. Captain Clark, 23 August 1804: "I walked on Shore and killed a fat Buck."

By the time, nearly a year later, that the expedition passed the northeast corner of the Helena Valley, the members' unbridled enthusiasm had sobered. The Louisiana Purchase and the land that was to become Montana might be a garden, but it was ungodly big, most of it painfully uncultivated. Clark again, July 19, 1805: "My feet is verry much brused and cut walking over the flint and constantly stuck full of prickley pear thorns. I pulled out 17 by the light of the fire tonight. Musqutors verry troublesome."

Later, just above the headwaters of the Missouri, things also got a little hungry in the Garden. Captain Lewis:

Nothing Killed today and our fresh meat is out. When we have a plenty of fresh meat I find it impossible to make the men take any care of it, or use it with the least frugallity. Tho' I expect that necessity will shortyly teach them this art. The mountains on both sides of the river at no great distance are very lofty.

The mountains again, a feature which would soon play havoc with Lewis and Clark and within only a few years of their passing become home to a small but vigorous group of white ruffians known to us today as Mountain Men. These trappers and hunters lived wild, primitive lives, and as they subdued everything in their path less wild than themselves, they also attained heroic stature in the eyes of civilized folks they had left behind. What they really did out here, of course, was live on the fat of an unspoiled land at the expense of everyone and everything in their way, leaving in their wake a legacy of death and disease. But they nonetheless became men whose skills with horse and rifle would be legendary, their lives embodying myths that often, unfortunately, overshadow the difference between the land they found and the land they left behind. We remember instead—or envision—the trappers as individuals ennobled by their primitive contact with nature, elevated in stature above the mortal yeomanry left sweating behind teams of mules in Missouri. And, because solitude and independence are vital parts of the Mountain Man mythology, we also tend to forget that the majority of them worked for a small number of highly exploitive companies, whose chief concern with wilderness—like most of the corporate profiteers who followed—was to extract, ruthlessly, a wealth of raw materials in exchange for profits to be spent in the East.

Even if we admit the arrogance and violence with which these gangs of professional killers approached the wilderness and its native populations, we still insist, in our imaginations at least, on glorifying qualities we know they must have had: resourcefulness, endurance, undeniable moments of courage, and above all (in the literary tradition of Fenimore Cooper's Natty Bumppo) remarkable skills with the rifle. They lived by and achieved dominance through this latest bit of technology, after all, and their ability to shoot became both part of our western mythology and identity to such a powerful extent that some Montanans still feel compelled to fire high-speed bullets into low-speed buffalo grazing out of Yellowstone Park … in the tradition of our mountain-man heritage, of course.

But listen to Osborne Russell and his account of a buffalo hunt near the Snake River in 1834:

> I now prepared myself for the first time in my life to kill meat for my supper with a Rifle. I had an elegant one but had little experience in useing it, I however approached the band of Buffaloe crawling on my hands and knees within about 80 yards of them then raised my body erect took aim and shot at a bull: at the crack of the gun the Buffaloe all ran off excepting the Bull which I had wounded, I then reloaded and shot as fast as I could until I had driven 25 bullets at, in and about him which was all that I had in my bullet pouch whilst the Bull still stood apparently riveted to the spot I watched him anxiously for half an hour in hopes of seeing him fall, but to no purpose, I was obliged to give it up as a bad job and retreat to our encampment without meat.

From the beginning then, an interesting set of discrepancies between actual experience on the frontier and the way we have since chosen to imagine that experience, has developed: a confusion of myth with history and of legend with literal event, which although potent has little to do with our contemporary lives in Montana. And these discrepancies between myths like the Noble Savage, the romantic primitive, or the happy agrarian yeoman of pastoralism and the brutal realities of both the land here and man's abuse of that land must be blamed to a large degree on writers; writers from outside the region who wrote mountains of fiction about experiences they had not shared and did not understand, while striving to create emotional responses, in a distant eastern audience, which they had not themselves earned. Certainly the worst and most voluminous example of this kind of writing was Erastus Beadle and his Dime Novel Series. Beadle—like the producers of the television series "The A Team"—realized that to make money as a publisher he would need to attract a mass audience with a standardized product. Beadle managed to perfect a series of formulas for adventure fiction based loosely on the romance and wilderness perils found in Fenimore Cooper's Leatherstocking Tales. And his dozens of books, often ghost-written in as few as three days, with such fanciful titles as *Baby Bess the Girl Gold Miner* and *Deadwood Dick's Dream*, sold like hotcakes.

Beadle's formula was, in fact, largely responsible for the transformation of one particular mountain-man figure, from inglorious hide-hunter to American hero, still remembered today as "Buffalo Bill" Cody—a character created by a distant mass medium pandering to the ignorance of a mass market audience. One of Beadle's most prolific writers, Prentiss Ingram, later became a staff publicity agent for Buffalo Bill, writing two hundred ostensibly factual stories about him. That Buffalo Bill in his old age became unable to distinguish between the actual events of his life and the fiction created by ghost writers about him foreshadowed the frailty of our collective Montana identity today.

As if to further complicate our situation, Hollywood arrived on the scene. And it was only a matter of further technological advancement from the stylized western characters of pulp novels to the stars of the Saturday-afternoon matinees who populated our childhoods with the desperate villains, melodramatic heroes, girls in distress, and peace-loving town folk of the Sixgun Romance. The formula for these B Westerns was essentially the same as Beadle's, although the horses ran even faster on film and the barrels of the hero's guns grew noticeably brighter.

On my father's ranch there's an old bunkhouse where some pretty real cowboys used to live. Before a friend and I remodeled it several years ago, 1930s vintage posters for the Cheyenne Frontier Days Rodeo, several bullet holes, and a dozen full-color movie magazine pictures still adorned the inside walls. Gene Autry hung there, wearing radon-bright blue jeans tucked into burgundy boots and a western shirt blazing with embroidered peacocks; Gene pointed a chromed sixgun off-camera while crouching beside a silver-inlaid saddle so heavy it bowed the top rails of his corral. Imagine the confusion among those men who worked for my wrangler grandfather. There they were, working cowboys and not a decent shirt among them, let alone chromed six-guns or saddles that would take a crane to move, yet hanging on their open-studded walls like mirrors were contemporary visions of what cowboys ought to be. Or could be, if they learned to sing. Of course the men who milked and rode and hayed for my grandfather understood the fiction of Gene's pose, but there was nevertheless a distance between real and ideal that almost certainly had as much to do with the Saturday-night bullet holes in the walls as the dozen or so whiskey bottles I found when I tore up the floor. And that same distance between what we experience in our routine lives in Montana today and the way that experience is reinterpreted has an awful lot to do with the writing that has lately sprung to life here, writing that resists the primitivism of mountain men, the romance of "saving the ranch," and a chivalric code that rides exclusively on horseflesh at the expense of "helpless" women.

Some time ago Wallace Stegner asserted that the West does not need to explore its myths much further. "It has already relied on them too long," he said. And of course he's right. For most of us today Montana has become a Western Twilight Zone where you can count the Minuteman missile silos as you drive the last thirty miles of gravel road to the Augusta Rodeo; where self-proclaimed mountain men snatch world-class women athletes, shoot up the posse, and retire into the wilderness to survive off the land undetected for six months; where commuting businessmen are as accustomed to see-ing cowhands on horseback moving cattle in the browngrass foothills above the interstate highways as the cowboys themselves are to microwaved bur-ritos and laser stereo discs; where our fastlane lives simply refute most of our western fantasies, whether they are inherited, mythological, or imported from Hollywood. And the contradictions between who we think we're supposed to be and who we seem to have become sometimes make us, as Tom McGuane says, "just a leetle crazy." In a place like this, dime-novel idealism just does not mix with real-life bad-time blues; every so often somebody goes out to the parking lot for a .44 magnum Peacemaker replica in a tragic attempt to sort out his troubles the old-fashioned way.

Drugs, food-stamp lines, AIDS, and the threat of nuclear meltdowns are facts of life for Montanans who still, at least in some secret recess of their imaginations, see themselves as isolated and independent and stolid as the winter hunters, line-shack herders, and singlejack prospectors of the last century. But few of us really do those things anymore, which makes our schizophrenic situation here all the more painful and unpredictable. Fact is, a whole lot of us sell stuff down at Wal-Mart or fry hamburgers for a living.

Amid this confusion, writers—some native to the state, others who moved in a few years back to stay, still more who migrate between here and someplace else—are today producing fiction set in Montana that focuses on this western chaos; fiction that probes our shaky sense of place and our wobbly sense of ourselves . . . our alternating lusts for open spaces and wider highways, for untamed wilderness and greater access. Writers appeared who have been crass and honest enough to write about what they really see here, wise enough, like Bill Kittredge and the late Richard Hugo, to understand and accept the desolation of small-town life and the vertigo of rural isolation; writers frank enough, like Richard Ford, to create characters whose only connection with landscape is to stare at it through the windows of an expensive, stolen car, and in no way be ennobled by the ride. There's Tom McGuane, who often drops his characters through a filter of new money into Montana towns like Livingston and lets them discover that for them there will be no enduring home in this place, no healing contact with land even if the land is right there waiting. New writers have appeared in the wings who bring more than education and a knack for words to their craft, authors like Neil McMahon, who understand the grinding weight as well as joy of working with one's back for a living, and poets like professional rodeo cowboy Paul Zarzyski who admit the pain of injury as well as the continuing passion to compete. There are even a couple of ranchers among this new bunch, although it's anybody's guess who let them in or how long they'll stay.

Many of Montana's new writers produce work that crosses traditional lines between genre fiction and serious fiction in settings as grand as the high Crazy Mountains and as grim as poolhall latrines. James Crumley's popular detective novels come to mind, where violence is balanced by an honest compassion for losers lost along the way, where something like love can pass between father and son on the front stoop of a country bar as well as a lesson on life's priorities. This scene, for example, from Crumley's newly re-released novel, *The Wrong Case*:

He came out behind me, a huge dark man smiling tiredly, a glass of neat whiskey in his large hand. With the first swallow, he rinsed out his mouth, then spit off the porch into the dust that rimmed the parking lot. The second, he drank, emptying the glass. Then he patted me on the head, perhaps sensing what I felt. Even at his drunkest, he was kind and perceptive, at least around me. As he held my head in his great hand, I was warm in the lingering sunset chill. . . . The fields, a lush, verdant green, grew dark with shadows, nearly as dark as the pine-thick ridges, but the sky above still glowed a bright, daylight blue. A single streak of clouds, like a long trail of smoke, angled away from the horizon, flaming a violet crimson at the far end as if it had been dipped in blood. But the middle was light pink and the end nearest us was an ashen gray.

"A lovely view, isn't it, son?"

"Yes, sir."

"But it's not enough," he said, smiling, then he walked back into the bar, laughing and shouting for whiskey, love, and laughter, leaving me suspended in the pellucid air.

Like Crumley, most contemporary Montana fiction writers concentrate on characters who ride not so much from the purple sage as from broken marriages, failed attempts to reinvent themselves, and overdue, unpayable debts. They seek not so much to tame the West as to find ways to face it. Many such characters don't make it, and what is most clear in their failures is that they are not heroes, but men and women struggling as best they can with contemporary problems in an extraordinary place. Caught between the extremes of complex urban society and the emptiness of rural isolation, these characters, like many of us, yo-yo between the two, as unable to enter society for long as to return home in any lasting way. No one brings this effort and the chilling possibility of failure into sharper focus than James Welch. From his first novel, *Winter in the Blood*:

> It could have been the country, the burnt prairie beneath a blazing sun, the pale green of the Milk River valley, the milky waters of the river, the sagebrush and cottonwoods, the dry, cracked gumbo flats. The country had created a distance as deep as it was empty, and the people accepted and treated each other with distance. But the distance I felt came not from country or people; it came from within me. I was as distant from myself as a hawk from the moon.

Perhaps these prodigals are Montana's truest present characters, embodying a longing most of us share for a connectedness to place and culture, an invitation to stay, or at least an honest welcome home. And so it is, that we struggle in our literature as in our lives with the distances within us and between us in our bittersweet attempts to connect with this place Montana.

My sincere thanks to Bill Kittredge and Bill Bevis for plowing the ground and planting the seeds for this essay.

Readings:

Adams, Robert, Lewis Baltz, and others. Landscape: Theory. New York: Lustrum Press, 1980.

Adams, Robert, Beauty in Photography: Essays in Defense of Traditional Values. New York: Aperture, 1981.

Adnan, Etal, and others. Russell Chatham. Seattle: Winn Books, 1984.

Broder, Patricia Janis. The American West: The Modern Vision. New York: Little, Brown, 1984.

Goetzmann, William H., and William N. Goetzmann, The West of the Imagination. New York: W. W. Norton, 1986.

Heidenreich, C. Adrian and Virginia L. Montana Landscape: One Hundred Years. Billings, Montana: Yellowstone Art Center, 1982.

Johnstone, Mark. "Landscape: Perceiving the Land as Image" in New Landscapes, James Alinder, editor. Carmel, California: The Friends of Photography, 1981.

Kittredge, William. Owning It All. St. Paul: Graywolf Press, 1987.

Martin, Russell, and Marc Barasch. Writers of the Purple Sage: An Anthology of Recent Western writing. New York: Viking Penguin, 1984.

McConnell, Gordon. A Montana Collection: 1985-1987 Recent Acquisitions by the Yellowstone Art Center. Billings, Montana: The Yellowstone Art Center, 1987.

Stegner, Wallace, and Richard W. Etulain. Conversations with Wallace Stegner on Western History and Literature. Salt Lake City: University of Utah Press, 1983.

Stegner, Wallace, and Page Stegner. American Places. Moscow, Idaho: University of Idaho Press, 1983.

Szarkowski, John. American Landscapes. New York: The Museum of Modern Art, 1981.

Trenton, Patricia, and Peter H. Hassrick. The Rocky Mountains: A Vision for Artists in the Nineteenth Century. Norman, Oklahoma: University of Oklahoma, 1983.

Whipple, Dan. "The Meaning of Landscape: Through the Eyes of Gary Bates." Northern Lights, Vol. II, No. 1, January/February 1986.

Montana Spaces 1988

DAMNED IF YOU DON'T

You know how it is. You see them on your way to work. Big bikes, covered with road dust, headed the other way—out of town. Or maybe there's just one; some lone wolf leaning back against his bedroll, wearing a pair of World War II Royal Belgian Flying Corps goggles, no helmet, what may have once been jeans, and a bandanna that needs an oil change. As he goes by, you look in the rearview. If his ride's got a license plate, it's so spattered with mud you can't make it out. That really bothers you.

And his bike: something old, Harley or European, maybe some duct tape holding the rotten seat together and a ripple of dents across the tank. The bike has that peculiar sound, too—an angry rock-and-roll you can't quite place until you pull onto the job site. But hell, it sounded just like that old Triumph or Harley or Norton you've got covered with broken lawn furniture and ruptured garden hose, collecting dust in the back of your garage. Didn't it?

Nothing happens for a few days. Then, without thinking, you buy a road atlas and a six-pack of off-brand beer at the neighborhood all-night store. You go home and begin studying the tiny blue lines of secondary highways in Idaho, Wyoming, Colorado, New Mexico—the ones as far from national parks, cities, recreation areas, and tourist traps as possible. Some of those blue lines you remember like fragments of a dream.

After the six-pack, you go out to the garage and flip on the lights. There it is—standing in a puddle of rancid oil, partly hidden under a roll of worn-out carpet. The tires are flat, the chromium alloy surfaces of the wheels and cases tarnished the color of gray hair. The remains of your scooter. As you clear away the accumulated junk around the machine, you notice that acid—from the battery that froze and burst a couple winters back, remember?—has eaten not only a hole in the concrete floor, but also through important things like wires, rubber bushings, gaskets, and most of the paint on the machine's lower end.

It crashes down on you and you don't fight back. There's what used to be your ride, looking like an archeological find. You're stunned, not only by the machine, but also by some sudden, revelations about the way you've let life put you in a box.

Sooner or later that urge you've never understood, but always recognize, comes back. It's a many-faced fiend that promises you everything. When it whispers to you at work you can't help yourself. You start making parts lists and figuring your pocket change real close (you'll have to skip the ol' support payment and the rent again this month). You sweat out dealin' with the boss, trying to get a couple of weeks off, then decide to just fuck it and quit. Out of the blue you remember who you loaned those roughed-out leather jeans to, just before you were drafted. You clean out the garage and start borrowing tools. But what the hell's behind this craziness that all of a sudden stampedes over the comfortable sanity you've cultivated ever since: 1) your ol' lady took off with the stereo and TV during your last trip; 2) your girlfriend split with your stash during your last trip; 3) you spent a week in a Nevada jail during your last trip; 4) you were fired and/ or evicted because of your last trip; 5) all of the above?

It could be a lot of things—a periodic need to re-invent yourself, a special vision or a dream that out there, on that ever unwinding ticker tape of asphalt, you're going to find the style and grace and romance of a secret place you've always known was waiting—an isolated canyon, lit with mad golds and purples, as if painted in your mind by Maxfield Parrish, where the woman you dreamed of as a child stands waiting beside the highway, for you.

Bullshit. You probably just want to get away from your rat-funk town, find some new country with great bars in unlikely places, ride your scooter all day, and get just a leetle loaded. Either way, early one morning you're going to kick that old knuckle-head alive, pull down your goggles, and notice—on the way out of town—some guy headed for work, who stares at you as you pass. Damned if you don't.

Because I was searching for something I couldn't name, I didn't plan on destinations. I had a vague notion of roads I might ride, country I'd like to see again, but little more. Why turn a quest into a bus schedule, right?

That first morning out I felt the kind of acceleration you'd expect from three mules and a pint of Wild Turkey. A few miles from town I turned off the Interstate and slalomed my scoot between the faded white center lines on the frontage road. It was tricky because of some foot-deep frost holes, fresh cow splatter, and scattered road kills. I found that the old reflexes had slowed some, that my reaction time was off. No problem. The sky was clear, there was no other traffic, the sun warmed the side of my face.

I remembered other trips, years ago, when I rode in the shadow of *Easy Rider*. The good old days of long aimless rides when I took fierce pride in running the only machine I could afford: a used 441 BSA Victor Special, whose megaton vibrations gave me kidney trouble for months, and, my bros claimed, some frontal-lobe damage as well.

Shortly after noon that first day I noticed thunderheads off in the southwest, dead ahead. I could feel the burgers and suds I'd sloshed down for lunch riding like mud in my guts. The cramps in my back had gotten so bad that my face went into muscle spasms. I'd been hanging onto the handlebars so hard in the steadily increasing wind that my hands had gone to sleep. And I noticed that the bike was making an unusual sound, a ticking, tapping, clanking that I couldn't remember ever hearing before.

By late afternoon I was beat. From there on it was just plain guts-ball endurance. The closest town was sixty miles away, across the most godforsaken country I'd seen since that accidental B-52 strike outside Dalhart, Texas, back in '72.

The strange noise in the bike jangled my concentration. I figured the worst: a bent pushrod that would have to be back-ordered from Cleveland or Prague or Vladivostok. But I didn't have to worry about the clouds anymore, because I'd been riding in a wind-driven arroyo-boiler for half an hour. Thanks to my years of experience and careful planning, there was just one thing I forgot to bring. My rain gear.

The endless sage-covered hills, gray as a breech-block to begin with, vanished behind curtains of wind-driven rain. I began to wish I was home, watching the roaches, knocking back some High Country Barley, and waiting for the ex to call about the late checks. But I made it. Some town I'd always confused with another one hundreds of miles away loomed up, looking sinister in the twilight. I couldn't believe that I'd wandered so far east. Although I'd planned on sleeping out there, in the sage and pines, I pulled into the first motel I saw and forked over a short stack to an old fart in slippers who didn't like my act at all.

The motel cut into my beer money, but I needed a shower, a place to dry my gear, somewhere to hide.

That first night out after a long layoff is probably universal. You wake with a start, staring wide-eyed at the television test pattern. It looks like some kind of sophisticated bomb-sight. You feel awful. Your ass is rodeo-sore and you're stiff all over. The evening you had planned to spend scouting around for a wild little beer joint was spent slouched in a chair, dreaming of oncoming semis and blown lower ends. Then you remember that rattle in your bike. You remember, too, as I did, that trip in '69, when the Victor seized up just north of Nogales and how it felt riding home broke on the Dog. And you relive the long cross-country trip when the tachometer cable went crazy, burning up, sounding like a thrown timing chain eighty miles south of Rock Springs. And you remember your luck, when later, in your relief that it had *only* been the tach cable, you'd wandered drunk through Rock Springs, counting cadence for no one in particular. And somehow lived.

The second day out I discovered that the rattle was actually loose tools under the seat buzzing against the frame. That was my last break, though. The rest of the week went down just like day one, only sometimes it rained harder in the afternoons. There were times when I remembered why I'd quit riding, all those years ago.

But I kept on heading south, the high plains gradually dried into something Western, and I found a couple of places that almost rang that bell I'd heard in my dreams: Elk Mountain, Wyoming, and Phantom Canyon, from Victor to Canon City, Colorado. My body got better, strength coming back into my arms with the miles.

South of Denver I got to rapping with the flag girl on a road crew. One thing led to another, and she introduced me to some bros in Durango. We took a weekend ride, up through Silverton and over the hump, through the snowbanks to Ouray. The flag girl's weight on my back fender seemed, as I thought it should, to lighten my load.

Later, I dropped in on some old friends I hadn't seen in a long time and crashed for a couple of days at their condo. They tolerated me while I worked on the scooter, but they talked too much about money and about how different things were now, how life had been better back in such-and-such. For them it *was* too late.

But on the road it ain't too late, no matter how long you've worked at the mill, to get it back together again, to get on your wheels and rediscover some dude in yourself you haven't seen for a long time. And, if you're real lucky, you might get a taste of what you hit the road to find. Those visions of road freedom—those fleeting moments of wild joy that come from scorching distance, alone and exposed—just might not, after all, be daydreams. Fact is, right now it all seems much closer to making sense, getting clearer, as if the answers wait just down the road a piece, beyond that next loping hill.

Easyriders 1984

Fall Fencing

Here, physical exertion matters.
It keeps me aware of what it means
to be alive, and what it costs.

—Teresa Jordan

I came home to Montana from Southeast Asia in September, 1974, intent on heading north with the woman who for some years had been the bright center of my life. But I dawdled, I hesitated, I lost my momentum. Instead of loading up my gear and driving away, I split wood for my folks at their place in the Helena Valley—one sharp day after another at the chopping block, working lodgepole and watching the Canada geese gang up in nearby wheat fields. In the evenings, Dad and I drove up to the ranch to spell my aunt Violet, who was caring for my ailing grandfather. I took to prowling the woods and fields, returning to the old log house only when darkness drove me in.

Late in the afternoon on the 6th of November, my grandfather lay down on the iron bed in the front room of the cabin where he had lived his whole adult life. "June," he said to my dad, "turn off the light and come over here and get hold of my hand." Dad drew up a chair, clasped his father's great hand in his, and in a moment the old man was dead. Right then the world changed. Just like that.

My grandfather had been in poor health for years, and despite my father's best efforts, the place had been dying, too. Roofs leaked, gate posts leaned; one barn was down, the cattle sold. Even the barbed wire fences, my grandfather's pride, had begun to collapse. It had never been much of a place, lying as it does in the hardrock hills along the eastern slope of the Divide, too dry and rough to really farm and too small to pay out as a ranch. Yet if my family has belonged to anything American, it has been to this place.

The day after the old man died, I cleaned out an unfinished cabin next door to the main house for myself and went to work making emergency fence repairs where our neighbor's black cattle were crossing downed wire. And each evening, as I sat on my bunk and worked Bag Balm into my swollen hands, I was one day closer to home. Those late autumn days with post bar and digger seemed to me as powerful and heady as good whiskey.

And they still do. Each fall, as part of our yearly cycle of jobs, I load a truck with treated posts and tools, steel posts and new barbed wire, and every morning for two or three weeks, I go out to rebuild fence. It needs to be done. But it's also an excuse to spend October in the woods, a chance to let life settle as the flights of geese and swans pull south, a time to touch the last real warmth of a sun that each day swings closer to the horizon and winter's storms.

This year the weather stayed fair into November, and I finished the season by replacing a portion of fence that crosses our upper meadow: four strands of badly rusted barbed wire overlapped with three feet of hog mesh, a fence so old, torn, and cobbled together that it was literally pulling itself down with its own weight. But because the original form and tightness had been lost long before I was born, there has always been for me something familiar and comforting and yet mysterious in its wild look. It crosses an area where I often played as a child, and maybe because of that I put off replacing it for at least a dozen years.

After eight decades, this particular stretch had come to have its own personality, containing an odd blend of materials and the specific marks of workmanship left by several different men. It had first been built at great cost in terms of hand labor and hard-to-come-by cash at a time when much else also needed to be done. Over the years it has been repaired many times, often with care, occasionally in haste. And I'd grown fond of it as it leaned these past years in that final stage of disrepair, the top wires slackened by jumping deer, the rotten posts leaning east and west. It was haphazard and beautiful and belonged to that place where the meadow narrows into stands of aspen, where frost-turned timothy marks the uncut borders of the fields, where thickets of wild rose and willow burn various dark shades of red. A warm and sheltered place, charmed by the sound of running water.

I began on the north side of the creek with a claw hammer and a tapered steel punch and worked south toward the leafless aspen along the creek, pulling staples from fir posts and piling the posts to one side to saw later for wood. For decades the common practice was to simply plant new posts beside old ones that had rotted off. Gradually, the posts accumulated until in places the fence came to look like a log palisade strung on wires.

One post had been squared in a crude sawmill, the semi-circular teeth marks still sharp against the weathered grain. And driven into a dovetail notch on one side, a square nail. This post had been carted here from somewhere else, an abandoned mine, perhaps, where it may have been part of a cabin or crib. Almost certainly it hadn't been part of a living tree for well over a hundred years. Twice used, it would, within the week, help warm our house.

Further on, driven into the top of a split cottonwood post, I discovered a .32 caliber Colt shell casing. The pistol that had fired it, I knew, belonged to my grandmother. Why the empty brass had been so saved or what its target might have been I could only guess. Blue grouse or a cottontail rabbit, likely, although the blues are gone now and the rabbits few and seldom seen.

Nearer the creek, the white skull of a horse hung from a cedar post that my granddad had dated by making a series of holes in the soft wood with a hammer and punch: 6/59.

Between the posts, fir staves had been stapled on to help space the various wires. Some of the staves had been pointed on top with a hand saw, so that each one seemed to have a little roof. Another of my grandfather's marks, another sign of his craft and workmanship and pride.

When I had the posts and staves pulled free, I worked back up the line with a mattock, chopping away wild rose and currant bushes that had grown intermeshed in the woven wire that had been added to the original fence by my neighbor's father, when, during the hungry Thirties, he'd raised hogs agile enough to outrun all but my granddad's wrath. Mr. Schuele had nailed up this wire net with one-inch staples, which my grandfather steadfastly refused to use, preferring to buy, even though the elbows and knees were forever out of his clothes, the more expensive two-inch variety. Although these two men had not been friends in life, they cooperated so successfully in maintaining the boundaries between them that their distinct, overlapping workmanship not only retained a unity, purpose, and individual identity long after their deaths, but eased the way for later generations to be good neighbors and friends.

As I rolled the old barbed wire into stiff, wagon wheel-sized hoops, the brittle strands broke each time I bent them back, yet where the wires broke, the metal inside still gleamed like new.

When I had lugged the wire out of the way, I was startled by how much the place was changed; the disarray of wire and wood, which my eye had grown so accustomed to, was gone. And with the fence removed, the meadow stood as open and continuous as it had before we came. A powerful image of an era had been erased; the evidence of our work there cleaned away as if that work had never been done. I looked a long time at that open piece of land, letting this fresh view—which I would soon alter again with a bright new fence—settle in my memory. For from where I stood to the snarl of aspen, alder, and willow along the creek itself, lay a narrow stretch of virgin land, untouched, because of the fence, by men and teams and plows, unaltered, as the meadows had been, by my great-grandfather, who had plowed up the skulls of buffalo, filled with rich loam like great horned cups, and the grooved slingrocks and stone hammers, too, that had felled them.

And I was reminded as I looked, because I had long ago been told, of a time fifty years before my memory began, of how, after the fields had been cleared of trees and rocks, after brush fires had burned for weeks and the stumps had been shot free with black powder, my great-grandfather and his twelve-year-old son had pressed the timothy seed of their first crop into the dirt by rolling a hollow pitch log around and around the field by hand. And, as each time I have mowed the land they planted, I was again reminded of how it was planted, of the poverty and determination, the strength and fatigue, the sweat and hope that accompanied its planting. And I experienced a fleeting moment of sudden and intense joy as I stood there. After the years of my labor in those fields, pushing that log has come to seem a part of my own life.

For the next few days I returned to the upper meadow to build the new fence, one which looks much like those along interstate highways—a fence that is tight and straight and strong, a forgettable fence with no real character of its own and no function but to keep my cows home.

I find myself thinking about my granddad in October, and the young lady I had planned to join up north. He has been gone twenty-five years; she is a professor of geology, I understand. I'm still fixing fence, although down in the actual creek channel, where the wild rose and currant and willow grow four and five feet tall, there is a hundred feet or so of the old line left, held up mostly by brush and a couple of pipe posts and luck. Someday, a fire or flood might clear it away too, but otherwise, unless it falls completely down and the creek becomes a fairway for cows and bulls, I think we'll just let it stand.

Modern Maturity 1992

ALL OVER AGAIN

Let us cross over the river
and rest in the shade of the trees.

—STONEWALL JACKSON

In some ways Montana is just a great big small town, isn't it? If we stay long enough and make any effort to get around, we sooner or later bump into old sidekicks, friends of friends, acquaintances of former lovers. This kind of far-flung conviviality can get uncomfortable once in a while, especially when it becomes clear that certain stories are still in circulation—those little episodes in our personal history that might just as well be laid to rest. At other times, though, these chance encounters are as welcome and moving as anything we could invent in our best dreams. In Montana it's still possible to drive down a forgotten stretch of highway or walk along a vaguely familiar street and be abruptly lifted from the present in such a way that allows us to embrace again a person, place, or object that once opened our hearts to the world.

And so it happened last spring, as Margaret and I were headed home after a week of scouting eastern Montana, when we decided to spend our last night in Harlowton. We were road numb and more than a little dazed from all the country we'd seen, and since it was a calm, bright evening, we stretched our legs after supper by walking the town, stopping on the veranda of the Graves Hotel and again to peek in windows at the Milwaukee Road Depot, then moseying through neighborhoods that seemed especially inviting in the shade of trees newly leafed, where the muted sounds of lawnmowers floated off toward the Musselshell riding high in its banks just below.

As we doubled back at the north edge of downtown we passed what looked to be a secondhand store. I would have walked on by, preoccupied, tired at the end of the day, but Margaret stopped and said, "Whoa now. Check these hubcaps!" I glanced in another window to find myself looking at a gas tank from a Matchless motorcycle resting on a ledge about six inches away. Beside it, another tank bore the AJS motorcycle marque in gold script on flawless black paint. I put my nose against the glass and cupped my hands around my eyes and hot dog! There was a big, angry-looking Matchless single standing beside a 650 Matchless twin. And another Matchless, this one with "tea-cup" valve covers! And an AJS dirt machine. And more. All together, there were nine English motorcycles in there, looking limber and quick and aggressive, even resting on their center stands beneath fine mantles of dust. I remember a faint mewling sound coming from my mouth, and something in my chest making an abrupt U-turn.

When we pulled up at eight o'clock the next morning, a man in a scuffed leather jacket was standing in the sunshine beside a Matchless 500 single, talking with a boy on a bicycle. It was Larry Steuben, owner of The Snowy Mountain Trading Post, about to leave for a ride before the wind came up. On the Matchless. Which might be a bit like taking a Packard Clipper for a spin before breakfast with the guys.

It was obvious that Larry wanted to get on the road, but after the boy pedaled off I had to ask if we could take just a quick look at the bikes on his showroom floor. The next thing I knew, I was running my hand over a 1964 G80CS Matchless 500 single in much the same way you'd touch a fast horse, and spilling my guts to Larry about my first English motorcycle, a Greeves 250 Challenger dirt machine that I wish to God I'd hidden in a garage somewhere instead of trading, as I had a dozen others, in that long string of motorcycles I owned and battered in my unchecked youth.

Another 500 Matchless, set up as a scrambler, stood on airless trials tires as if waiting for someone to reattach its carburetor and exhaust pipe. A project bike but close to complete. And in a dim rear corner, an immaculate "Harris" Matchless with its dull black Rotax engine and transmission, looked awful fast just standing still.

We moved from motorcycle to motorcycle, Larry commenting on their pedigree and vintage. He called the 500cc single-piston engines "thumpers" and "big singles" and "stump pullers"; said "coming up on the cam" when he meant accelerate and "skinning kitties" for powering a motorcycle in a tight circle. And as I listened and let my fingers glide over handlebars and tanks, side cases, and frames, I wondered how it could be possible to think of machinery of such unsayable quality as obsolete. Would we ever think of that moment when we fell for the first time seriously in love as dated or as an event in the past which no longer touched our present? I sure hope not. Of course the more obvious question was this: How could we have abandoned this iron of pure delight for the cheesy luster and bug-like voice of the Yamaha?

As we looked at his motorcycles, Larry told us a little about himself, about growing up in Pennsylvania, the kind of kid who set pins in the local bowling alley during the winters and stacked hay in the summers for wages that went into his first motorcycle venture, a new Schwinn Panther bicycle that cost a hundred and ten dollars, and a sixty-five dollar "Whizzer" kit to motorize the Panther. He was fourteen when he got it bolted together and running. And it did run, a contraption that went thirty-five miles an hour under power, yet could be switched off and pedaled if a patrol car happened by. The cops looked the other way, and Larry ripped around town for a few months until he spun the connecting rod inserts on the crankshaft. Larry tore the engine down and replaced the factory inserts with pieces of bacon rind in much the same way his grandad kept a worn-out Model A Ford running during the Depression. Larry changed rinds in his Whizzer every couple of months until a fella went by one day on a Matchless. Right then the earth beneath Larry's feet slipped and shifted.

When he was seventeen, Larry bought a 1947 Harley 45 from a neighbor whose daughter had filled the gas tank with sand. He got it running and in short order traded it and the Whizzer-powered Schwinn for a 1951 BSA B33. Finally, he had a real motorcycle, one that let him do all sorts of riding from touring the countryside to racing in enduros and competing in hillclimbs. On a dare, Larry rode the BSA down a twenty-seven-mile stretch of brand new asphalt from Central City to Archer, Nebraska, standing on the seat with his arms outspread like wings.

For some of us, the names of certain English motorcycles still ring with authority. BSA, Triumph, Norton. Royal Enfield, AJS, Matchless. There resides in those names and marques that which has to do with raw masculine strength balanced with grace; in the appearance of the motorcycles themselves, a beauty tempered by the suggestion of violence barely restrained. Think of a cavalry saber sheathed in its scabbard, or a .455 Webley-Wilkinson Pryse displayed beneath glass. It's funny, though. Many of the great English motorcycle companies got their start in much the same way Larry Steuben's Whizzer/Schwinn came together. In the late 1890s, reckless young men with too much time on their hands began bolting gasoline engines into bicycle frames and roaring off through the bucolic English countryside with no brakes, no suspension, no mufflers, and, we have to assume, no fear.

The first Triumph motorcycles were built by marrying a two-horsepower Minerva engine with a bicycle frame and wheels. In 1905, Triumph began making their own power plants, beginning with a 360cc side-valve engine on the order of the Briggs and Stratton engines we see on wood splitters and sump pumps today. Birmingham Small Arms got its start in 1862, when fourteen gunsmiths who had formed a company to supply weapons for British forces during the Crimean War—hence the company's famous three-stacked-rifles logo. In the 1880s, BSA began making bicycles, and in 1903, the same year Orville and Wilbur skimmed above the grass at Kitty Hawk, the company added motors.

Albert John Stevens built his first gasoline engine in 1897 and continued to improve its design until 1909, when he and his three brothers formed the A J Stevens (AJS) Company. Their first production motorcycle featured a 292cc side-valve engine and a two-speed transmission. In similar fashion, a family named Collier, which had been manufacturing bicycles since 1878, built their first motorcycle in 1902, and, with an understatement typical of their day, called the thing Matchless.

Larry Steuben wasn't the first young fella in America to have his head turned by those slim, muscular machines crossing the water from Great Britain. But, like several generations of us, he fell hard in love with them in a way that would change his life. In January, 1965, Larry and his sweetheart happened across a motorcycle dealership in Fort Collins, Colorado, where a Matchless G12CSR stood on the showroom floor gleaming with chrome and rich black paint, a big red M beside each knee-knocker badge. Larry saw that machine and went just a leetle goofy. He immediately sold his faithful BSA and rushed to the nearest bank to beg a loan. Since he was working construction and on the move following jobs, the banker turned him down. "But hey," the guy in the suit said, "it would be a whole different story if you were married."

The opposing forces of capitalism and motorcycle lust put Larry in a hammerlock of desire. He was so crazed by his need for the Matchless that he asked his girlfriend to marry him right there in the bank. Of course by the time the young couple unsnarled the red tape involved with getting married, got their blood tests, and did the paperwork at the bank for their loan, the Matchless had been sold, snapped up by someone else.

Larry managed to buy his BSA back, raced on weekends, and tried to act like a responsible family man until 1967, when he happened across a new Matchless G15CSR in Lee Cowie's Motor Sport shop in Saint Louis. He traded his Beezer and some cash for the Matchless, quit racing, and rode the motorcycle of his dreams just about everywhere except to church.

Motorcycle stories are not, regrettably, all sweetness and glory, as Larry Steuben can tell you. In 1979 he was forced to sell the Matchless to pay for a divorce he didn't want. Eight years later his brother was killed on the same machine. Larry bought what remained of the Matchless from his brother's widow. Since then he has struggled to restore it, one impossible-to-find part at a time, in what can only be seen as a labor of love.

The Snowy Mountain Trading Post has several personalities. Besides the showroom, where the Matchless motorcycles stand aimed at the street, an adjoining space overflows with second-hand goods ranging from reloading equipment to a candle shaped like a Swiss cheese, complete with mouse. If you are in the market for an Astra toaster or a fleshing beam or some used crutches, this is the place. Margaret seemed especially dazzled by a Triceratops doorstop made from globules of melted lead and a set of flipper hubcaps featuring a completely chromed naked lady. Larry asked if we wanted to see his "other motorcycles" then led us into an eerie warehouse-sized chamber that revealed itself to be an elephant's graveyard of oil-stained steel and blown head gaskets, a great dim place where just about any motorcycle you could dream up stood handlebar to handlebar with other relics, in rows half a city block long, just waiting to be rediscovered and loved again by fools like us.

There they were, street machines and motocrossers with names now all but forgotten: a Jawa-CZ, sans engine, and a Road Toad; four Hodaka Super Rats in a row; a Zundapp; a Penton with a KTM power plant; and lots of cratered Japanese stuff from the Seventies and Eighties. The sheer volume of basket cases, bent frames and knobby tires sort of took my breath away, leaving me with a sensation not unlike what some guys might feel walking into an airplane hangar filled to the rafters with cocaine and Cuban cigars. I could have spent a weekend in there straddling ruptured seats, trying kick starters and front forks, twisting throttles and making little noises with my lips, lost in that shrine to motorcycles in an unlikely small town in Montana, a community whose best days may have passed with the displacement of another kind of machinery, back when the Milwaukee Rail Road pulled up its rails and quit.

When the Muses come after you, they really pour it on. Margaret and I arrived home to find an advance copy of Fred Haefele's new book, *Rebuilding the Indian,* waiting in our stack of unopened mail. I read it quickly the first time through, goaded by this saga of a fifty-one-year-old ex-professor tree surgeon, "in the mood to do something foolish." What Fred does is buy and restore a basket case, 1941 Indian Chief motorcycle, not exactly a job for the cautious or mechanically challenged. Just the Indian's lubrication chart on the book's inside covers would run most guys off, the old Chief a machine thirsty for oil, with more grease zerks than a John Deere baler.

Rebuilding the Indian is a *Zen and the Art of Motorcycle Maintenance* for grownups who appreciate craftsmanship more than philosophy. It's laid back, smart, and funny, a book about rediscovering enthusiasm by a man who sorts out his personal history while bringing a fine piece of American machinery back to life. Fred's story got under my skin, I admit, got me daydreaming about possibilities.

I should point out, right here, that American motorcycles, the Harleys and Indians, while worshiped by tens of thousands of loyal admirers, have little in common with the great British bikes. The two really can't be compared objectively or without prejudice. Suffice it to say, then, that 74-cubic-inch American motorcycles seem puffy and soft to some of us, fat boys at the prom when compared to those welterweight singles and hard-bodied twins from England.

The world-wide success of the British motorcycles overshadows the fact that with the exception of a few good years, following each world war, the companies themselves were often pretty shaky propositions. They were continually absorbing one another or going into receivership, so it's sometimes hard to now tell who built what. In the early Thirties, for example, Matchless acquired AJS. In 1937 Matchless Motor Cycles merged with Norton, Francis-Barnett, and James to become Associated Motor Cycles. AJS and Matchless then became sister companies, the machines in some cases identical except for their colors (blue for AJS, red for Matchless) and their tank badges.

The engineers stayed busy, and the mechanical technology evolved quickly. Overhead-valve engines had become common in the 1930s, and, pressured by the influences of European motorcycle racing, BSA, Matchless, and Triumph developed machines that were both durable and extremely fast, motorcycles that completely dominated world-class racing. At the 1955 Isle of Man TT races, 33 of 37 entries were BSA Gold Stars.

Although BSA, Triumph, Norton, and Matchless served as the foundation of some fearsome racing machinery, lightweight two-stroke bikes made by CZ and Husqvarna, Bultaco and Greeves began overrunning the big four-strokes in the mid-Sixties. Then, inexpensive Japanese machines got a toehold among American riders who wanted reliable bikes that were easy to start and didn't leak oil all over the living room carpet. By 1970 the English motorcycle companies were in trouble. Between 1971 and 1973, BSA and Triumph went broke.

The commonly-shared view among our older folks during the 1950s and early 1960s, that motorcycles were mostly about bad behavior, rebellion, and leather jackets with half-a-dozen zippers, was, of course, aggravated by Hollywood when Marlon Brando and Lee Marvin and their boys smashed up that little town in "The Wild One." After watching those stumblebums in action, what responsible parent would allow a growing boy to get anywhere near a motorcycle? In other words, for some of us it wasn't real easy getting started.

My first two-wheeler didn't even look like a motorcycle. It was a Mustang trail scooter with tractor-lug tires front and rear, a Briggs and Stratton engine with a kick starter, and a three-speed transmission. The footpegs were placed way up front so the rider couldn't stand to absorb punishment, which was unfortunate because it had no suspension whatsoever. But it would cowtrail in mud and climb about anything you'd try, all the while sounding like a badly abused lawn mower. I bought it second hand and pretty much destroyed it in six months.

During my travels on the Mustang I began to see guys who were riding actual motorcycles out in the woods. There were English Cottons, BSA Gold

Stars, a terrifying Norton Atlas, and those crazy two-stroke enduro machines, featuring an aluminum I-beam as the front half of their frames, called the Greeves. Watching them blast past through the pines in a fog of Castrol oil smoke made me feel foolish and small, a boy shamed by his puny Tote-Goat-like thing. So I did what I had to do.

I got an after-school job washing bakery pans at the local Albertson's store. Each pan was hidden under carbonized layers of sweetroll goo, and there were hundreds of them leaning in columns that reached halfway to the ceiling. My 300-pound boss, the baker, had let them go for a few months, but that didn't stop him from braying in a piercing, high-pitched voice that he needed clean ones *Right Now*! It was four hours of Hell, six nights a week. But a few months later I rode a new Honda 305 scrambler out the door of Red Drennon's motorcycle shop in Helena, a man at last.

On Sundays, a hundred or so riders would gather in the foothills of the Belt Mountains near Hauser Dam to chase each other down endless trails that had been carved in the shale by knobby tires. I joined them or tried to, sometimes having to shut down my Honda and listen in order to discover which way they'd gone. I rode the 305 to work, to school, all over the ranch, and, a couple times late at night, up the state Capitol's front steps. It was not quite a basket case when I traded it, three months later, for the new, ultra-fast Honda CB450, which I soon modified with trials tires and a sixty-two-tooth rear sprocket. I also took a hacksaw to the rear fender to give the bike a more chiseled look. Suffice it to say that I learned to ride by going as fast as I could until I peeled off and gravity took over. I was hard on machinery, but I put my head down, washed those pans, stacked hay, and worked a full-time job at the local smelter so I could keep trading motorcycles with Red.

To some of us young bucks, Red Drennon was all a man in full could be. He was cool and crafty and good-looking in a Clint Eastwood kind of way, a natural athlete who'd won some big endurance races, including the famous Paul Bunyan. Red was always going off on adventures like flying to California to watch the Swedes ride. He came home with the first Panama straw hat I'd ever seen and dated girls who were actual airline stewardesses. In short, Red was everything we required in a hero, a hero who had a lot more to do with that leap toward freedom Steve McQueen made on his motorcycle in *The Great Escape* than anything Marlon Brando could suggest.

In 1968 I moved on at last to what I considered a genuinely serious motorcycle, an almost-new Greeves Challenger. The Greeves was extreme in every way, crude as a stone ax, and, at only 220 pounds, with a 12:1 compression ratio corked by a radical expansion-chamber exhaust, a real heartpounder. I learned to jump logs and powerslide and in no time at all was casually riding up a plank into my pickup at the end of the day just like the rest of those Sunday afternoon hotshots.

Hard-pressed for basic transportation at the beginning of my senior year in college I traded the Greeves for a BSA 441 Victor Special. The Victor got me to class in Bozeman and to part-time jobs, and I fell in love with its deep, throaty voice and the gobs of low-end torque the big single churned out. I taught myself to loft the front wheel (with my feet up on the pegs) when a stop light turned green; to Thump Thump Thump across the intersection on the hind wheel, then ease back down, catch second gear, and continue on my way as if nothing had happened. The slow-motion wheelie was my one good trick. People in cars going the other way would turn their heads and gape, and I could imagine for a moment that I looked like Torsten Hallman or Peter Fonda.

The BSA got away from me and the US Army got me, and I eventually found myself in Lawton, Oklahoma, starting all over. I needed transportation out to Fort Sill each day, so I bought one of those bellowing Kawasaki triples. A year later, when it became clear my companion and I wanted to cover lots of ground with the relative ease of a road machine, I purchased my last motorcycle, a BMW R600. The beemer was wide and awkward around town: the gears clunked, there was a disconcerting amount of drive-line snatch, plus, the machine felt like there was an anvil atop the handlebars when the six-gallon gas tank was full. And it was littered with gizmos that seemed designed to trip a man up. More than once I coasted to a stop at a traffic light, put my left leg down until the cuff of my bellbottoms caught the tickler rod on the carb, then, unable to reach the ground with my foot, fell slowly over to crash while standing at a complete stop. People going the other way in cars would turn their heads and stare.

But on two-lane highways with lots of hills and sweeping curves, that BMW turned into a swan with great big lungs. The mirrors smoothed out around seventy, and with the steering damper screwed down, I would ride mile after mile with my hands in my jacket pockets, steering with my knees. At speed, the BMW had the stability of a gyroscope, and it was more than possible to achieve a kind of grace. Some of the most vivid moments of my life were spent in the vacuum created by the headlight fairing, the slightest pressure of Miss Roberts' hand on my hip telling me without reservation that there is love in this life, and that all the world's roads had been built just for us.

In the mid-Eighties my companion and I parted ways, and I sold the R600, a gesture, I suppose, aimed at settling down. Now, like Fred Haefele and Larry Steuben and thousands of other guys our age, I find myself a little stunned at having passed the big Five-O, and somewhat surprised, I guess, to be thinking about motorcycles again, as if they might be a way to postpone the inevitable, if not quite a means to recapture youth.

Ever since I met Larry Steuben and saw his Matchless motorcycles, I've been having a recurring daydream. In this reverie, Ted Turner and I walk through a factory about the size of Butte. I am wearing a white lab jacket. I have many calipers and pens. Ted has purchased the rights to the Birmingham Small Arms motorcycle name and marque and has spared no expense to tool up this facility to build original BSA singles and twins. He has created a vast network of dealerships across the country and sells each unit at close to a break-even price so most of us can afford one. Ted waves his Stetson at completed bikes rolling off the line and says, "This is great for Montana. Just beats the heck out of mining with cyanide." As Head of Quality Control, I couldn't agree more.

In Harlowton, reality cuts a little closer to the bone. Every other store-front along the intersecting main streets is boarded up, burned out, silent. The movie theater and the stately Graves stand empty except for ghosts. In Harlo, there's not much shaking, even on a Friday night, with the exception of two girls in a platinum Corvette.

Larry Steuben seems like a down-to-earth kind of guy. He has a regular job working for a powerline contractor, yet he's always on the lookout for flashes of chrome that might turn out to be an English bike, constantly talking long distance with collectors, or working on motorcycles in his shop. During our second visit, Larry admits to a little fantasy of his own. If money was not an issue, he says, he'd call Les Harris in England and arrange to buy the Matchless marque. Then he would acquire the empty railroad roundhouse in Harlo and turn it into a factory that, one, manufactures parts for vintage Matchless motorcycles, and two, produces a line of ultra-modern racing machines. "We'd put this town back on its feet," Larry says with a smile that lifts his beard and lights his eyes. "You bet we would."

Our choice of motorcycles as a means of transportation, and our preference for one breed or another are matters of taste, an inclination toward, or a desire for, a certain style. Those of us who love British motorcycles should remember that they were temperamental and required the kind of constant attention some special women demand. They leaked oil and dripped gasoline and would hurt you if you didn't master the exactly correct starting ritual. And most of them had those awful seats that looked like a squashed loaf of bread. But, bless them, they were a way of leaping beyond the confining boundaries of conservative small towns and the family farm, and we needed them just as badly as we needed our heroes and a chance to fall in love.

Larry thinks that some of us imprint like baby ducks at the sight of a certain motorcycle, then chase that image the rest of our lives. Well, maybe. We darn sure know the real thing when we see it, though. You bet we do.

I'm going to keep in touch with Larry Steuben. And I'll give Red Drennon a call one of these days, just to see how he's been. My former companion is a professor now. I need to track her down and talk about certain trips and listen to her laugh. And I plan to let my finest dreams pull me toward this: Some evening, when the wind lies down and the leaves go quiet among the trees, I will kick a big single awake. I will clunk it into first with the heel of my boot and turn up the wick and let the motorcycle carry me off toward those secret lands of innocence and hope; to the phantom canyons and mountain passes, lit with mad golds and deep lavenders as if painted in my mind by Maxfield Parrish, where the woman I dreamed of as a child cuts the evening air with me. We will cross a bridge at great height above a river and accelerate toward an instant of bright discovery that we always knew lay waiting, like the end of time itself, just beyond the next loping hill.

Big Sky Journal 1999

At Rest

I want to weep for questions
I never had the sense to ask . . .
There are stories I want to know
which are irrevocably lost.

—WILLIAM KITTREDGE

I can hear a Saturday branding getting underway as I step from my pickup at the wrought-iron gate to the Radersburg Cemetery. It had rained before dawn, and although the sky has cleared, the air is heavy with moisture and the smell of burnt grass from the ditches. Down along Crow Creek toward the Missouri the faint voices of riders carry above the drone of cows bawling for calves. And as the May sun warms me through my shirt, I want for a moment to be down there with them in the noise and grit of their long day.

I have been drawn during the past few years to the heart of this valley, to its open farmland and brushy bottoms, its stony horse pastures and hidden sloughs where the great sandhill cranes come to nest. One paved road runs west up the Crow Creek Valley from Highway 287, following the old freighter's trail from Toston toward the Elkhorn Mountains and the nearly-abandoned mining town of Radersburg. Country lanes wander north and south from the main road, leading to ranches sheltered among groves of cottonwood trees. On the extreme southern horizon, the shimmering snows of the Tobacco Roots seem like a mirage of mountains or an aperture in the sky. This is jack fence country, where red-winged blackbirds sway on cattails, where an occasional pheasant will sprint across the road. And since there is seldom any traffic, it's possible to slow down and open yourself and let the country take you in.

I am haunted by this valley in my dreams and by those of my blood people who once lived here. They have been gone from this place for seventy years; their names and the labors they accomplished are all but lost. Their land has passed to others, their houses and barns to ashes and dust. Yet I feel them here as if sensing a presence among shadows, and I find something like solace among them in this place where they once thrived.

Lately I've begun to spend more time with people who have receded into the past and with places that exist nowhere as they once were, except in the nightland of my dreams. And I'm coming to see that only in memory and dreams do those places and people still live. I want to believe that by repeating the names of the dead I can postpone their final disappearance. Some of the dead I want to claim as my own.

This is a family plot, then, in the prairied foothills of Montana: my mother's father and his people. I am the only one who visits them now. Once each spring and sometimes in the fall I come and sit among their stones. This is not about grief. It is about a need to touch that which resides in me that came from them, about reaching back in place and time to catch a glimmer of them here. That I could have known more about these people but asked so little twists my heart.

The cemetery stands on a bald hill overlooking Earl and Pauline Webb's hayfields and the fields of their neighbors as they spread across flat land to the south and east, a fine and gentle view with foothills backshadowed in distance above the line of cottonwoods tracing the creek. A handsome country, productive and open to sky. Fenced with barbed wire, the land inside the graveyard is the same as the pasturing hills beyond, land overgrown with bunchgrass, lupine, tumbleweeds, and sage. Scattered among the stones, a few shrubs, some thirsty lilacs, but no pretense of lawn grass whatsoever. Just inside the front gate, an outhouse leans in long disuse, its door not quite shut.

Curlews pass overhead on set wings, gliding toward the fields below, which once belonged to Earl Webb's grandfather, a man who kept a new set of plow reins blacked and polished and coiled on a peg in the ranch kitchen. Those reins were used for only one job—to lower coffins into the ground where I stand. I turn in a slow circle, trying to imagine living at a time in this place when people lowered their dead with plowlines, when they dug into the earth with a pick and shovel to make room for a neighbor's child, a sweetheart, a father, a friend. I think of lingering until the final words of comfort have blown away, to fill the hole again.

Some of the markers are round-topped slabs of wood, the legends they once bore long since sanded smooth by wind. A few stones have fallen as the ground beneath them settled; several have broken in half. Hearts shaped from woven strands of barbed wire lean against two stones; on some graves plastic flowers have been anchored with rocks against the wind. Old men lie beside infants whose limestone markers bear the faint figure of a child at peace with lion and lamb—so many children among the oldest stones, whose epitaphs and embossed angels' wings have faded with their memory. "At Rest." "Gone But Not Forgotten." "Gone Home."

Meadowlarks court among the monuments and sage, sporting in the early light. One, standing atop the limestone spire of William Davis' monument, stretches his neck, and, after a false start, lets go the pure rift and warble of Montana spring, music as clear and startling to me at that moment as it must have once been to the man lying there. My mother's great-grandfather, and beside him his wife, the family matriarch, Jane Morgan Davis. Their son Thomas is buried here, and beside him, his son, George. Their daughter, Annie, and her pioneer husband, D.T. Williams, complete the row, two families connected by marriage and affection and buried head to heel. Of the six neglected Davis graves, one remains unmarked and unknown, although someone years ago circled it with fragments of broken brick.

They were farmers and stockmen and the wives and children of farmers and stockmen, come all this way from their native Wales. What promise the valley must have held for these families when they arrived in the early 1870s: rich bottomland and vast, open pastures; sweet water and enough rain, and scores of miners at work in the nearby hills, who needed to be fed. Once a farmer got dug in, he could sell every egg and potato, every pint of milk and pound of meat he and his family could produce. And at premium prices. Why, they could even haul water to the dry boom town of Radersburg in their spare time for a dollar a barrel. These first families made money, and they put that money into more land and ditches to carry their water, into tools and implements and stock. For the Davis and Williams clan the promise of the valley was quickly realized—their original places doubled in size, and during the coming years, doubled again.

Jane and William Davis left Wales in 1851. They farmed in Iowa, and hauled freight in Nevada and Utah until they followed their daughter and son-in-law to Montana in 1875. They were not homesteaders, although they would later add land by homesteading. William Davis bought land that had first been deeded to a private soldier named Zachariah Felton as "bounty land" for his services in the Georgia Militia, during the Cherokee Indian Removal of 1838. Felton did not come to Montana Territory and his claim reverted to the government. When William Davis acquired Private Felton's land in April 1876, the transfer of deed was undersigned by President Grant. During the next twenty years the family bought additional parcels from the Northern Pacific Railroad as it liquidated portions of its land-grant holdings, and they paid cash for extensive ditch and water rights held by the very first settlers in the valley.

The thrill of their safe arrival in the Montana territory must have been overshadowed by the last of the Indian Campaigns. Only four months after William Davis' first land patent was signed, Colonel Custer made a serious error in judgment at the Little Big Horn. The Bozeman Trail, which had been abandoned because of Red Cloud's War in 1868 was not reopened until 1877. In August of that year, Chief Joseph's retreating band encountered a group of white sightseers from Radersburg in what is today Yellowstone National Park.

The Indians kept the whites with them for two weeks then released them well-traveled but unharmed. It is a pretty notion to think that these Crow Creek Welshmen, who came from the southern border county of Glamorganshire and for generations had known the weight of the Englishman's boot, felt some empathy for the plains Indian. It is likely they did not. Equidistant from the raw towns of Butte and Helena and Fort Ellis at Bozeman, the Crow Creek settlers were on their own.

The first beef cattle in the valley were almost certainly Shorthorns trailed up from Utah in company with bull teams pulling wagonloads of plows and stoves and seed, and those cattle thrived in the unfenced hills at the foot of the Elkhorn Mountains, where they were driven each spring to pasture until the fall gathering commenced before the first big storms. Even as domestic cattle increased in numbers, herds of buffalo still grazed the Missouri River bottoms. Unlike the rancher barons to the north and east, the Crow Creek families fenced their holdings and put up hay against winter. The weight their animals gained turned into dollars that bought harrows, mowing machines, and rakes; sawmills, harness, hand tools and nails. They and their neighbors built squat log cabins roofed with poles and dirt, and log barns with open mows to shelter their horses and hay. They raised a surplus of chickens and pigs, and fed the hogs with skim from the cows they milked and with the excess of potatoes and grain they harvested each year. These were dirt-floor folk who worked with soil and water, animals and wood, but by 1890 frame houses with verandas were rising as testament of a people who had created a bounty from hard work and the blessing of good land.

It was a good life if you didn't weaken, but distance and weather and hard work took a toll on people that is now way beyond our imagining. People were found dead where they gave out on their way home. Loners like Billy Davis were found frozen in their cabins. Teams of horses were felled by lightning in the fields, as were the men who worked them. The only roads were gumbo ruts that turned to mush in wet weather, when wagons, mired to the axles, were left standing in their tracks until the road dried or froze. God help you if you needed a doctor.

People suffered at home. Young women died in childbirth and their children were taken by diseases of every kind; men were maimed in their work, and their injuries, if not immediately fatal, led to gangrene and amputation or the lifelong misery of broken bones poorly set. The strain of isolation bore down on people, and there were those who succumbed to melancholia and others to fits of rage and violence, while others still came to this hill by way of their own hand.

Cause of death notations in local cemetery logs: kicked by horse; typhoid fever; shot; meningitis; womb trouble; horse fall; diphtheria epidemic; summer complaint; consumption; dropsy; explosion of black powder; heart failure following miscarriage; measles; green fever; hit by bucket; exposure; dementia; neglect.

They lie on this hill now, friends and neighbors and enemies together, and their names yet ring of homelands beyond the sea, people beyond all means of reconcile or return: Doughty and Holdaway, Hossfeld and Poe, Easterly, Ralls, Kitto, and Greaves.

I stoop down and rest on my knees to pull weeds from around the stones. The centers of the graves have been mounded with gravel, heaped on like an afterthought as they settled. I could remember coming here as a child in the Fifties, vague, black-and-white memories of grey afternoons when my dad and I wandered among the stones while my mother put flowers on her father's grave and stood with him a while. He was not part of our lives, and I had felt no connection to him or this place. The visits to the cemetery were something to be endured until they ended and we were free to drive into the mountains to fish the little creeks for rainbows. As I got older and found excuses to be elsewhere, my folks came here by themselves.

In the spring of 1981 a flash flood washed out hundreds of miles of roads in central Montana. I worked that summer and fall as an equipment operator on a crew repairing roads in the Helena National Forest. In November we went to upper Crow Creek to salvage a timbered bridge that had been lifted and carried downstream and deposited six feet off the ground between two old cottonwood trees. The crew quit early one Friday afternoon, and I followed with a flatbed truck loaded with timbers and decking. I had plenty of time and on impulse stopped at the Radersburg store and asked directions to the cemetery, where I had only to look a few minutes before finding my grandfather's stone. The sky was clear and sharp, the cemetery ridge and valley, a glory of light and color. As I looked out on the country in the solitude and peace of that moment, I felt myself touched by something that resided there, a presence or memory that was part of me and alive within me. Beyond the barbed wire lay a country of great beauty, and in the ground at my feet lay stones bearing the names of people who had belonged to that country. Their last name was my mother's maiden name, and although I had not known they were there, I understood that I was standing in a consecrated place among my people.

Before I left I drew a diagram of the Davis and Williams plots and made a list of the names and dates on each of the stones, and I penciled in the location of the graves in the Davis plot which had no stones or markers. A limestone spire, William Davis, 1816/1890; a blue granite slab, Jane Davis, 1818/1904; the unmarked graves; and a flat stone for George Davis, 1888/1926.

Next to the Davis family, on an ornate block of granite, which is the largest monument in the cemetery: David Thomas Williams, 1835/1904. Annie Davis Williams, 1844/1904. Beside them, five of their children in a row: Thomas died in 1875, at age three; David in 1883, age three; and Nellie in 1885, age three. Edward Williams lived ten years, six months and died in 1885; his sister Hattie, 19 years, seven months, passed in 1887. Nellie and Edward died one day apart. Of ten children, five lived, and their children's grandchildren raise livestock in the valley still.

On the way to Helena that afternoon, I was filled with the excitement of unexpected discovery as well as the realization of my own great ignorance. I had been immersed for years in stories about my dad's people, those long-boned Saxons who first came to Montana during the homestead rush of 1909. But here, all of a sudden, were kin who went back to the very beginning of white settlement in Montana, people who got here in wagons or on horseback or on foot. And I knew nothing of them or about them.

That evening I drove to my parents' place in the Helena Valley and had my mother sit down with me at the kitchen table. I showed her the diagrams I'd drawn, the names and dates. "Who are they?" I asked. Because the dates on the stones didn't seem to make chronological sense I asked, "Who were your grandparents? Are they the people in the unmarked graves?"

My mother shook her head. She could remember her father when she'd been a child, she said, and yes, we were related to the Crow Creek Williams family. She and the actress Myrna (Williams) Loy, were second cousins. She did not know her grandfather's name, although she remembered a woman named Hyatt who had apparently been her grandmother. "How could that be, if your father's last name was Davis?" I asked. She said she didn't know.

I suppose I was carried away by a sense of discovery and wanted quick, easy answers. But the more I asked my mother the less she would say, until finally she folded her hands in her lap and looked at them. I was astonished at her reticence and the sadness in her face. She was the most open and generous of people, but there she sat with her jaw clenched. My mother's mother, Emma, who had died only the year before, would have known those people or known about them, and because we were the best of friends, she would have told me everything. Everything.

My discovery of the Crow Creek/Radersburg graves created a great riddle for me, one that has lingered as a dull ache ever since. Over the next few years I coaxed bits of my mother's past from her, random, seemingly unconnected incidents and events that nonetheless revealed more and more about her childhood, as well as hinting at the kind of man her father, George Davis, had been. She was born, she told me, on an isolated ranch on Ray Creek in the Belt Mountains, where her parents had gone for safety during the Influenza plague of 1918. The doctor who was supposed to assist her birth arrived in a buggy, in the middle of the night, four hours after she was born. I imagine him exhausted, dazed by the failure of his science and all the dying in his town, where, after the ground froze, corpses were said to have been wrapped in canvas shrouds and stacked like wood until the ground thawed. Twenty million people died of Spanish Influenza. But there in the lamplight in a cabin on Ray

Creek, Montana, a girl child named Ellen Louise Davis was delivered into life with no help from the outside world, no aid from anyone but her mother and father.

Her memories seemed vague and scattered as if the family had lived on several places in only a few years. She remembered a frame house on a ranch near Crow Creek where her father brought home gunny sacks full of ducks he'd shot on the Missouri River. Another place, where she played outside in a yard of packed dirt. She had no idea where those houses were located, only that they were on established family ranches. She recalled that her father had been a railroad man before she was born, that he'd courted her mother by taking Emma along on local runs in the cabs of steam locomotives while he worked. Imagine that: An engineer at the throttle as chaperone; George, a suitor in pin-striped coveralls, shoveling coal into the maw of the boiler; and Emma, a narrow-waisted girl standing beside an open window, carried away by romance and steam as Montana clacked past at impossible speeds.

My mother remembered how George had taken them to Independence, Missouri when she was six years old and that they stayed for two years while he studied electronics. And she told me how, when he completed his course in the spring of 1926, he bought two new Model-T Fords, which he and Emma then drove home to Montana. It was an adventure, an overland automobile trip across the American West before surfaced roads. They wore goggles and dusters while they drove, and they slept out at night. They stopped often to wait while George fixed flat tires or made mechanical repairs. Sometimes they followed roads that took them off in the wrong direction, because they could find none going in the right one. But they made it. They should have come home like heroes of conquered distance and gone on with life. Instead, they discovered that their house, which George had rented to cousins while they were away, had been demolished. The cousins had burned their furniture in the stove and left the doors open so that cattle had come inside and walked holes in the floor. Swallows darted through broken windows, tending mud and wattle nests on the parlor walls.

The ruined house must have been some kind of fulcrum for George Davis, giving leverage to a feeling of negligence or defeat that loomed larger than any simple loss of property. When my mother spoke of her father, she thought of him as a handsome, expansive man, a responsible and talented man. But always as we talked, I could feel behind her words how their lives had turned, how everything had gone wrong.

Years later I would discover his obituary in a bound volume of *Townsend Star* newspapers. It is inconsistent with his death certificate and contains several factual errors. But this much seems to have been more or less true: On the eleventh of July, 1926, he left his seat on the front porch of a house belonging to a family named Gruber, people who lived nearby and were, in fact, his cousins. He walked through the house and went outside behind the house and shot himself through the head. My mother was in the front yard with other children when she heard the blast.

Kneeling at his grave, I feel a pressure against my hip. I thumb George Davis' gold Hamilton from my watch pocket and weigh it in my hand. Each minute is numbered on its face, the ornate hands that continue to mark time, blue-black. In studio portrait postcards made in 1910, the chain and fob belonging to this watch cross his chest. He was twenty-two years old the day he sent one of those postcards to Miss Emma Bessette, the girl who would become my grandmother. In blue pencil he wrote on the back, "Your loving sweetheart, George Wm Davis." In that pose he seems to radiate an elegance and poise no one else in my family has possessed, a young man of genuine potential, clean-featured and mild, sober and direct. I wouldn't mind one bit being him.

He was a child of the age of the railroad in Montana; born only a year after the completion of the Northern Pacific line to Helena in 1887, he left the isolation of ranch life as soon as he could for a job on the line. He was a man who embraced technology, a man whose short life spanned the decline of the horse, the victory of steam, and the ascendency of the gasoline engine. In 1910 he was a locomotive hostler and fireman for the Northern Pacific, living in a rooming house right across the street from the NP Depot in Helena. That same year he was a member of the Montana State Rifle Team, choosing to compete with the brand new, bolt-action Springfield rifle. And he put his rail-road wages into an Indian motorcycle with sidecar, which he rode to Butte to see Emma. In 1910 George Davis was a young man who could cover distance, a prime man with real possibilities and all of life ahead.

I put the Hamilton in the bunchgrass beside his stone and watch the second hand sweep its own small circle. He must have been very proud of it, for it is as finely made as the one love of his life. She was only fifteen when she received his portrait postcard, sixteen when they were married, a black-haired beauty barely five feet tall, a slim girl of vast energy who liked to laugh. In the photographs that survive of her during the time of their courtship it is easy to see why a young man would risk a hundred miles of mud on a motorcycle for an afternoon with her. In her eyes there is a calm, unschooled intelligence; in her mouth, the frank suggestion of a yearning to kiss.

In her old age, my grandmother once told my father, with a laugh and a gleam in her eye, that she and George made love until dawn their first married night together. When I started riding motorcycles, she told me that once during their courtship, George lost control of the mighty Indian on a gravel road and upset the machine and its sidecar in a ditch. She was pinned under the sidecar, and before he could lift it from her, its weight pressed a gold locket she was wearing into her chest. She carried the faint scar the rest of her life, and she wore the locket, which contained a twist of his hair, until her death. Fifty years after he shot himself, she loved that young man and grieved for him. After all those years and twenty more besides, his pocket watch keeps perfect time, although time has taken those lovers away.

After my parents' deaths in the late Eighties, I began to visit the Radersburg Cemetery more often, usually as a side trip on the way to somewhere else, sometimes when lazy Sunday morning drives seemed to lead me there by chance. Still, it wasn't until the early Nineties that I found myself in the Broadwater County Courthouse with a legal pad and a list of questions. A week later I left carrying a briefcase filled with photocopies of hand-written deeds, abstracts, and indentures; census lists, death certificates, and bills of sale. I taped together quad maps of the valley and plotted out the properties the Davis family had owned. Gradually, as I read and reread the documents, a broad outline of their lives there began to emerge. Clearly Jane and William Davis, the first generation, were in the livestock business. Although married, they used formal legal instruments to lend and borrow money back and forth between themselves. William owned their land and a portion of their water rights. Jane owned their cattle and the rights to certain ditches. Jane handled most of their money and owned land of her own, as well as the family brand, a "D" on the right shoulder. From the 1880 census I learned that in addition to their married daughter, Annie, they had two sons living at home, Thomas, aged 22 and William Jr., aged 20. There was also a hired man on their place named Scott Watter.

In 1883 my great-grandfather, Thomas Davis, borrowed money from his father and bought land from the Northern Pacific Railroad to start his own place. The next year, Jane Davis sold 180 head of cattle and paid off Thomas' mortgage to her husband in return for a $1600 mortgage on her son's land. Around and around they went, continuing to borrow and lend, buy and sell among themselves until Jane died in 1904. They seem to have been an insular family, people who did business among themselves and kept the lawyers busy. Language may have been a barrier to the larger community; Jane and William may not have been able to read or write in English. Jane may have been completely illiterate, or, as one rumor has it, blind, since she made "her mark" on all documents with an X. If they were more comfortable speaking Welsh than English, they were still shrewd bargainers. They were not cowboys, although they did much of their work from horses; they were never big operators, but they steadily acquired land and water until, by the late 1890s, they owned and worked three separate ranches that made use of irrigation.

William Jr. worked with his brother until Thomas married. I lose track of young William in Lewistown in 1912. So, finally, there is my great-grandfather, Thomas Davis, married to Augusta Wittick in the mid-1880s, father to George Wm in 1888, and divorced by 1890.

By bits and pieces I was able to fill in blanks, link names with dates and locations. Yet even such simple detective work made my belly hurt, made me wake with a start in the middle of the night feeling that I was on the very edge of discovery. The more I learned, of course, the more I wanted to know. The paper trail that took me to Tom Davis stopped in 1911 as if he had up and quit the country. And I could still not fathom how my mother had known nothing at all about him.

I also noticed a certain reticence among local people I spoke with, and, since I'm shy about bothering country people who don't know me, first-hand research didn't take me far. Then, almost by accident, I found myself talking with Wallace Turman, a beautiful old man who had grown up in the valley and ranched there all his life and was, at ninety, a living repository of local history. Like many old-time Montanans, Wallace referred to places by the names of the original owners, so that no matter how long those people had been gone, their names remained. When I mentioned my grandfather and that he had been a suicide on the old Antonetti Place, Wallace shook his head. "There were *two,*" he said. "*Two* suicides there in that family."

And I began to see it, the unmarked graves, the way Thomas disappeared in documents and records, the way some people seemed to close up. When I spoke his name, Wallace nodded vigorously, "I was there when the Sheriff came," he said. When I asked if he could give me the year, he closed his eyes, seeing, I supposed, the mayhem of that bloody morning in his childhood. "It was 1912," he said with certainty. "Davis went out there to get $500 that Joe Gruber owed him. Us kids went around to the back porch where the Sheriff washed up afterwards, and there was hair and chips of bone and teeth around the basin."

Within a few days I had copies of Tom Davis' death certificate and obituary. It was just as Wallace had said. Tom Davis was supposed to have shot himself at first light, April 29, 1912. According to the obituary, he had a large funeral attended by all pioneer families and was buried in the Radersburg Cemetery. His obituary also reports that he left $15,000 cash money and several ranch properties in his estate, a considerable accomplishment for a man with almost no education who seems to have worked alone most of his life. But how strange to make public his financial affairs while there is no mention of him at all in the cemetery log.

Why would that prosperous man lie in an unmarked grave so long among his own? What feelings or lack of feelings were at work in his only son's heart that George Davis would inherit his father's wealth yet not put down a stone bearing his name? Was Tom Davis such a bad man? Had he been a sharpie, a chiseler, a cheat? Had others paid for his success, or was it simply that the stigma of suicide was so strong, the shame so great, that the unspoken wish of the community was to leave him on this hill to be forgotten? Whatever the reasons, there is no excuse for unmarked graves, and it nettles me, although I have since put down an engraved granite slab with his name and dates and the word: *Stockman*. Still, I ended up taking my best guess at which of the unmarked graves was his.

What passions ruled and ruined him I can only guess at too, although I know he was a hard man given to accumulation, a lone man whose nature kept him isolated and apart. He had divorced, something rare at that time among those people. Land prices had skyrocketed with the influx of homesteaders on dryland after 1909, and Tom Davis was cashing out. In 1911 he sold two ranches, selling and buying back another in a three-way scheme within two days. He does not seem to have been actively ranching at the time of his death. Without his own ground to walk on he must have gotten lost.

In the one photograph of him that remains I see the jaw and stance of a scrapper, a hard-nosed Welshman who knew how to make a dollar and keep it. And there on his chest is the gold chain and fob that his son would later wear in his postcard portrait, and that I would one day play with when I was a child. But isn't there a hint of humor in the man, something in his posture that suggests amusement or affection for his son, George, the gawky boy holding a Winchester rifle cradled in his arms? And look: Although it is only about 1905 and an outhouse stands in the background, they pose beside an automobile with wooden spokes in the wheels, their automobile. The boy is shy and awkward, although he already has the large hands and heavy wrists of a hard worker. A lifelong lover of firearms, he is so obviously proud of his rifle.

Far off in the distance I can see the gliding wink and shine of glass and chrome from the highway as the traffic of America hurtles on, the present so compelling, the speed of life so great, that the past fades away like smoke. When I look at Tom and George Davis in their snap-brimmed caps and muddy shoes, my eyes sting with frustration. I am drawn to them with the force of pumping blood, and I want to step into the photograph and stand unnoticed behind them with a hand lightly touching each man's back so I might feel them breathing. I want to intervene, to step between them and onrushing time even as meadowlarks call and curlews glide past above our heads. I want to warn them against the emptiness they will leave behind. I want to let them know that someone will remember them with pride. I want to tell them to fight back, to make the other son-of-a-bitch bleed instead; I want to tell them to never give up, to wait for me. I want to hear their voices.

I slip the Hamilton into my pocket and get to my feet. The mild light of late morning touches my face and the monuments of my people. The gold chain and fob have been lost and no one cares. From here I can see a plot of land that belongs to me—ten dollars' worth of ground beside the gate in the back fence. The wind that bends the bunchgrass there scrubs away at epitaphs; someday the stones will all be smooth. If there is tragedy here, it is in the loss of stories. Their stories could have brought them back, don't you see, because stories outshine instruments of gold. Stories outlast stone.

Big Sky Journal 1998

Part II
Fiction

From *The Blind Corral*

Harley stepped onto the porch where I'd taken to smoking after supper. He latched the door and tugged on the visor of his railroad cap: a relief pitcher about to enter the last home game. "Let's go for a drive, Pilgrim," he said, eyeing the cattle too. "Seeing as how you're supposed to be working for me, I figure to get some work out of you. Wood room's empty. Come on, I'll show you some snags you can buck up."

We headed for the south end of the place, where Harley's father had homesteaded first. I drove slow, stopping now and then to look at the dead trees Harley pointed out. They stood alone, above timber of a later growth, their brittle limbs scraping an empty sky.

We followed cow trails in and out of the timber, through parks and hay fields, occasionally seeing the white rumps of mule deer moving off through scattered bull pine. We criss-crossed his neglected hay fields, overgrown now with Ranger alfalfa and a variety of wheat grasses. Until Summerfield and I had been in grade school, Harley had grain-farmed this land. Even if we had been too young to be much help, we'd picked rock and harrowed a lot of weekends that our little buddies spent at the Y shooting baskets.

Dry-land farming, celebrated now only by rusting tin signs nailed to decaying sheds: "This farm uses the Ferguson System." Each fall, turn the land under, two furrows at a time, and in the spring, disk the earth to death; pick rock for days, then harrow it across the grain, breathing the fine dust that worked deep into bearings and teeth, distributors and lungs, wiring and eyes. How many times had I seen my father working on the stalled Ford tractor, in wind that cut through any cloth made, his hands black and his face dark with rage?

I didn't see how plowing and planting could have been done with horses on such a scale in such rough country. But for much of three men's lives it had been done; the horses dragged the implements until the iron wore out, and places were named where favorites had died in harness. A rock pile for Old Frank, a dry wash for Conn, a stand of pine later, for Conn's mate, Kelly. Places honored by naming, hallowed by the memory of what it was to die pulling a plow.

For the last fifteen years, Harley had cultivated alfalfa hay, and each year now it came of itself. Each spring we towed a drag of railroad iron and tractor tires around the fields to spread mole hills, level gopher mounds, and break up manure. We pulled it with a pickup, and in a good day a man could cover forty acres, out of the wind and dust, listening to the radio or reading a paperback.

We topped a rocky point and saw a three-quarter-ton truck parked beside the boundary fence. A lone man worked the ratchet handle on a wire stretcher. He straightened when he heard us, then bent again to join the rusty strands. I pulled opposite his outfit and killed the engine.

"What say, Easy Money?" Ted Schillings asked, his blue eyes bright as neon in his ruddy, wind-burned face. Not a big man, he got as much done in a day as anyone. The years of labor showed, though, in the slope of his shoulders, the curve of his bent back. Yet he worked on alone, even into the dusk, doing what he knew ought to be done.

Harley and I got out and faced him across the fence. Ted's father and Harley had not been friends. Although we got along fine, there was a clouded past, a sense of clans that never went completely away, a distance we didn't try to narrow.

"Those survey crews just go where they want." Ted gestured with his cutters at the end of a rusted wire. The tip showed the bright bite of pliers.

Harley took the wire in his hand and looked at it with mild interest. "Wonder what they're up to now?" he asked.

"Must have needed to back-shoot a reference point from somewhere in your place, Harley. They've been hanging ribbon from the Kennedy Flat to the head of Jackson this week. Looks like a used-car lot above my meadows."

Harley looked off toward Sheep Mountain, then back to Ted. "Won't be long, they'll have us surrounded."

Ted put his tools in the clutter of cedar posts and wire, saws and shovels, axes and hammers heaped in his truck. He brought a yellow folder from the cab and, with his finger, drew a circle on a blueprint-like map. "Five-acre lots," he said. "All of Rocker and Clark's Creek clear to the highway. They been down to see you yet?"

"Not lately," Harley answered. "And I don't expect to see them either. You heard what they're pulling on Amy?"

Ted nodded and placed the map back in the folder. "They write big checks that don't bounce," he said, his thoughts flickering across his face. He noticed the wire stretcher hanging where he'd left it when we'd driven up. "Bigger checks than a dozen lifetimes on my place could cover."

"I want to show you something. Pull up over there." Harley pointed toward a fenced enclosure where we had stacked rye hay when he first bought a baler. We had used army-surplus hospital tents to cover the stacks, and ragged chunks of rotten canvas still flapped on the barbed wire fence.

"See that snag?" Harley aimed his finger at a burled, limbless log wedged between two boulders. "My dad and I cut that. Bottom was full of ants was why we didn't take it all." He looked at the ax marks that still showed where limbs had been lopped off, then closed his eyes. "We stopped for a smoke that morning," he said. "Sat down on a rock for a few minutes over there to rest. Well, sir, one of those big black carpenter ants had crawled up the inside of my coveralls," Harley's eyes snapped open, "and he bit me right on the head of my pecker!"

Harley laughed a laugh too deep to come from his sunken chest. I chuckled too, seeing him in my imagination, coming off the rock, his kid's eyes wild. "Ran halfway to the creek before I got my pants down. Hollered most of the way— made such a sudden racket, me yelling and my dad laughing, that we spooked the team. They busted loose and took off for the barn. When I sulled back up here, with my bottom lip stuck out, the old man took one look at me and started in all over again. Laughed himself right down to his hands and knees." Tears ran down my grandfather's cheeks from laughing. "God, but I missed that man," he said. "After he did himself in."

Harley began to cough. He struggled for breath, got it, and coughed again. When the spasms passed, he wiped his eyes. "That was one of the few times I recall him ever letting go. He was usually such a hard case—reminded me a lot of your dad."

He cleared his throat, chuckled, and said, "Leave that one go. There's plenty of dead wood around." He seemed to consider something for a minute, then climbed from the truck and waved for me to follow. Partly hidden by the butt of the old snag and completely surrounded by clumps of buck-brush stood a flat stone with an X chiseled across its surface. Harley knelt before it and drew his fingers along the chipped, intersecting lines. "This is what they were looking for, the surveyors. The section corner that centers this end of the place." He touched the stone again as if it were a holy relic and added, "You might need to know where it is someday, Pilgrim."

Autumn had been on a long, sweet roll. In the meadows along Jackson Creek the aspen had completely turned; their dry leaves quivered in the light morning breeze like spotted yellow tinsel. Withered Dutch clover sparkled each morning under melting frost, and when the frost burned away, it turned a brilliant green. Stripped by the first storm, the alders rattled, stark and silver among the reds of wild rose and willow which had overgrown neglected portions of the meadows. And in the timber, pine tags turned an inviting warm tan.

On my knees, I watched as the old snag above me tipped, its brittle limbs twitching from the vibration of the saw, until, cut completely through, it stepped off its stump. As it fell, it pivoted a graceful quarter turn, seeming to hang for a moment, suspended between earth and sky.

I waited for the dust and flying sticks to settle, then climbed onto the butt and walked the length of the tree, limbing it close to the trunk with Harley's ancient Mall saw. Red rot churned from the teeth on the spinning chain and floated away on the exhaust. Straining against the weight and torque of the gear-driven saw, I began to buck the log into fourteen-inch blocks.

The clean October light blued valleys below, yet seemed to amplify mountains rising along the horizon, light that intensified the reds and yellows in pine bark, magnifying the gemlike amber in each bead of pitch and sharpening the unlikely Day-Glo colors of lichen clinging to the dark sides of trees. Even the granite, that dull and most enduring feature of the land, sparkled as light shot through its minerals, flakes of mica sparkling like mirrors. I pulled off my shirt and let the sun warm my back.

I sawed the stump flat for a chopping block and began splitting wood. Elegantly simple, the work gave my hands occupation and my mind a freedom to wander. The sky above me seemed to crackle with light—as it had that October when she and I had headed south through the heart of British Columbia, taking our time, towing her horse trailer to the last, late shows of the season. Evenings we camped as far from roads as we could, so taken with the country that when we woke in the mornings, it was sometimes with a sense of wonder—as we had once near Revelstoke, encased in cold nylon sleeping bags, shivering in the morning chill and each other's heat, when we heard the first lonesome honks and saw them coming in low over the lake, flying between mist and the mirrorlike water, so close we could see their eyes: the first fast flights of migrating Canada geese.

I hadn't gone looking for war; it came to me that autumn, when Summer was shot down in the Highlands. In another month the light here would darken, trees would turn dull again between the layered grays of stone and sky.

Calluses had formed along the base of my fingers. I could feel strength coming back into my hands, strength so gradually reduced I'd only missed it after it had gone. I turned a block so the fine crack across its top was opposite me and drove the splitting maul through the barely visible line to the heart. The stillness around me broke as blasts at the new Kaiser quarry to the north echoed back off the Elkhorns. Each day they drilled and dynamited further into the earth, their charges reverberating from the hills. My hands ached from the saw and maul, and I remembered that the grip I'd had at twenty-two began to ebb at Fort Sill. "Hands-on training," they called it, a faster way to make cannon cockers, even though the war was winding down. Sergeant Major Lewis, cool and black as obsidian: *Run those trainees out to the range their first day, put 'em on the guns, make them shoot till dark, then run 'em back here for chow.*

I split the wood fine, for Harley's kitchen range, and stacked the pieces in the box of his pickup. Another distant blast rolled off the mountains, echoing back to me like the Sergeant Major's hip voice . . . *When they hit the classroom after that, they'll KNOW what those level bubbles are for.*

October, bright and fine, the worst of the killing summer heat behind us and a new training cycle under way. Six nameless trainees standing in a nervous half-circle behind the split trails on my howitzer, facing me and Garrett on that open, sun-warmed Oklahoma hillside. Four complete batteries, trucks, a mess tent, commo wires running off through scrub oak to forward observer outposts. The hills we aim at would have been good to ride, low and rolling, open to sky.

The side of Harley's pickup had warmed in the sun. I rested my naked back against the metal, remembering how she was to have arrived that same day from Canada, remembering Garrett's hillbilly voice—*You better speak up, young man, when you're answerin' me*—as we started our new charges on basics, making them take turns—COUNT OFF!—burying the spades that anchor the gun against recoil. I show them one at a time how to place powder bags in the slim brass canisters, how to mount the sleek, high-explosive projectiles on the canisters, how fuses are screwed into the hollow threaded noses of the projos, explaining how a clock in the fuse starts when the round is fired. And I tell them how the fuse determines exactly where a round explodes, how each fuse can be set to burst the charge aboveground or impact detonate when the projo strikes the ground; even be adjusted to delay until the projectile has buried itself underground. "Bad guys in bunkers and spider holes don't much like that delayed fuse," I tell my trainees, and they grin, growing cocky already, beginning to believe.

Sweat trickled down my chest, although I hadn't moved in several minutes. *Stop. You can stop this right now.* But when it comes, it comes of itself, as if memory has a will of its own. My off-post running buddy and co-instructor, Drill Sergeant Billy Garrett, swinging into his act, harassing each new man from every sudden angle . . . *So don't be fumble-fartin' around dropping those fuses, you read me, son?* . . . keeping them shook and awake, and when I good-cop them, they gravitate to me, listening and learning, anything to avoid his haunted eyes and lashing tongue. She was coming to stay, and I had been in a frenzy of cleaning my off-post apartment, buying furnishings I wouldn't have bought for myself. Even as I elevate and traverse the barrel, spinning the cranks on the left side of the gun, I wonder where she is on the road. Garrett and I have the trainees level the gun bubbles over and over, until a cherry second lieutenant checks the piece with his gunnery quadrant, then off to one side asks me if he has the number of mills right.

I explain the commands that will soon come: QUADRANT, how high; DEFLECTION, how wide; SHELL, high explosive, beehive, Willy Peter; FUSE, how long; CHARGE, how much powder. I show one man at a time how to push a complete round into the tube with a clenched fist, show him how the sliding breech block will actually push his fist away. "It will push your fist but not your fingers," I tell him. "Remember that or you'll be writing Jody left-handed letters." More tight grins as they carry projectiles in the crooks of their arms, each of them feeling the thrill of loading.

I shivered from the sweat chilled on my back and noticed wood chips scattered around the chopping block at my feet. *If only I had been paying attention, instead of thinking about you.* I touched the place where the purple scar ran along the side of my jaw. Off south, beyond the fields and timberline, as far away perhaps as the old Prim place, I heard a barking dog, then another and another.

We insert rubber earplugs and the world becomes deadly and mute. The long-delayed order for smoke comes; we cover our ears and open our mouths; one trainee on each of the sixteen howitzers rams a round into the breech, another runs the block closed, jerks the triggering lanyard, and we have rounds in the air. Every gun jumps, rubber tires bounce off the ground; recoil mechanisms flash back and the projectiles hurtle away: Look! You can see them! Brief dots against the October sky and they're gone in a ringing snap of stretched steel and the slamming impact of muzzle blast.

Dogs, running in the timber to the south, barking, frenzied, chasing something. Barking.

My trainees are stunned by the violence that is to become their craft. They look at each other like homesick boys. The rounds do not strike the ridge we watch but impact a mile beyond, where, finally, we see the faint trail of dust and smoke, and later hear what sounds like summer thunder. In three months those kids would have been good, good enough to hit a Vespa three miles away.

I listened to the dogs growing fainter, then bent, touched my toes a few times, and tried to shake the cramps from my trembling hands.

Viking/Penguin Press 1986

LADY

From *Lady*, a novel in progress

The power of the dead is that we think they see us all the time.
The dead have a presence . . .
They are also in the ground, of course, asleep and crumbling.
Perhaps we are what they dream.

—DON DELILLO

WHITE NOISE

In the upland meadow where his ditch met Blanchard Creek, Clayton Horn cranked his headgate open and watched the water churn to foam in the discharge box beneath his feet. The water sped off down his ditch, clearing as it went, to a lucent, glacial green. When the gate was all the way up, Horn leaned his forearms on the iron spokes of the bullwheel and looked out into the swollen race of the upstream channel where an ouzel dipped on a stone. Its mate darted past through the sunlit mist, singing as it flew.

Horn felt clearheaded for what seemed the first time in months. He had walked the four-mile length of the Jack Mountain ditch that morning, throwing rocks and windfalls from its bottom, checking talus-slope flumes for leaks, and patching spots where game had worn away the downhill banks. It was a job he'd done since childhood, a trip he looked forward to during the last dark months of winter, a day that usually meant spring had finally come. Yet on the upper reaches of the ditch, in shaded stands of fir, he had stopped several times to shovel paths for his water, through knee-deep drifts of half-rotten snow.

It was an old claim, this water, and although the people who had dug the ditch were gone, in Horn at least, something of them remained. He was taller and by degree fairer than most of the mixed-bloods thereabouts, yet the *Métis* features were plain in his face: high cheeks and aquiline nose, strong mouth and mahogany skin. Still, his eyes were grey, and there was that English cleft in his chin.

A drop of sweat fell from his nose to the back of one hand, and Horn straightened to unbutton his blanket coat. For the third time that day he took a postcard from the left breast pocket, unfolded it, and looked at the cover, where a camel stood amid endless dunes, bathed in burnt-orange desert light. Horn smiled. He shook his head. On the other side, in a hand he knew as well as he knew his own, "By the time you get this, I'll be back. Love, V." Horn refolded the card and buttoned it away, wondering just where she was.

In the opening around him, frost-turned timothy shined in the midday sun. Thickets of wild rose and dogwood burned various dark shades of red. It was a warm and sheltered place, charmed by the music of running water. Upstream, Blanchard Creek swung south into stands of withered spruce. Above the trees, Horn could see part of the Rocky Mountain Front, peaks—worn by wind and kerfed by ice—rising grey and white against atomic blue.

Horn looked into the high country until his eyes watered, then turned and looked north toward home. Five miles away the plains began. And between that region of stone at his back and the yaw of space ahead, there lay a band of grassed and wooded hills, a countryside of meadowlands and basins between extremes, a verdant place, the center of the world.

Horn glanced at the sun. He took one last look around the meadow and noticed that the ouzels had gone. He closed the headgate halfway, picked up his shovel, and walked down the ditch bank until he was ahead of the first flow. He dropped into the ditch itself, a few yards ahead of the advancing foam, swinging along fast, and listening to the whisper of water as it followed him down the mountain toward his fields.

In openings where the ditch crossed sidehill parks, Horn could see out to the very edge of the Earth, fifty miles to the north, where the Great Plains curved away toward Canada. Dust rose along the horizon there, augering east on twisting winds over saffron strips of dryland wheat. Among the groves of winter-bowed aspen, though, with only the faint sound of his spade tapping cadence on the stones ahead, Horn felt absolutely alone. But the clarity of April light among the trees—interspersed with glimmers of mountain-shaded grasslands below—was not enough to satisfy him. Light and country and his own company had been for a long time exactly enough. But as he approached forty, Horn was surprised to discover that he was no longer happy with what he had. During the past winter he had struggled to pin down the restlessness that rode him for days at a time, trying to single out what had gone wrong. The closest he could come to an honest answer was to admit he wanted something new, some change that might accelerate his life or elevate his soul.

He had been daydreaming along for a mile when he saw a tan slash of color in the budding trees above him, and he took several steps before he realized that it was a bear, feeding on the move, occupied with what lay in its own immediate path.

Horn stopped. He eased the tip of his shovel into the hillside beside him and leaned against the handle for balance. He watched as the animal quartered downhill, rummaging among last year's leaves, casting its broad, dish-faced head for scent. It looked his way, and Horn turned wooden: an alder snag lodged in mud.

The bear rolled a log and dug at the redrot along its bottom, pausing its hunchbacked labor to lick bugs from runnels in the decay. For all its size, it breakfasted with slow grace, seeming at thirty yards almost reserved. Horn waited, the rounded tip of handle pressing against his chest, feathers of wind touching the short hairs on his neck. When the bear sat back on its haunches to scratch, Horn took a long slow breath.

The water caught up to him with a hiss. It hesitated at his boots, deepened, and ran along its course without him. He tucked his chin and watched it ladder up his laces, inching to the frayed cuffs of his pants, darkening the cloth and climbing on to clinch his calves like block ice when it topped the bullhide boots. Horn sucked air through his teeth and watched the hillside above him for cubs.

The bear got up, shook itself, and gazed around near-sightedly, as if waiting for an idea. It rubbed against a tree; it opened its mouth and seemed to yawn. *Sometimes*, Horn thought, and gave in to the tremors telegraphing through his thighs, *you eat the bear*. His stomach cramped with adrenaline, and the muscles in his shoulders quivered with chills. He gripped the hardwood handle and clamped his jaw to quiet his teeth. *And sometimes . . . .* He waited, the water tugging at his legs, the bear lazing toward him through the scrub. By the time the bear smelled the water, Horn's lower legs had gone numb as roots.

It came down through aspen, disappearing into thickets of snow-brush and emerging again in a clatter of dry leaves and sticks, shouldering along, its hump and back silvered by the sun. Fifteen yards from the ditch, a Franklin grouse broke cover. It churned from a clump of juniper at the bear's feet and flew straight at Horn's face, clucking and pounding the air in panic. As the bird passed overhead, its wingwind touching him, Horn found himself locked eye to eye with a timeworn female grizzly that looked to weigh almost, even all gaunted-out, as much as an average yearling steer.

The bear stood slack-jawed, lower lip sagging from worn front teeth, in an open-mouthed attitude of surprise. She studied him with small umber eyes, and Horn felt that gaze flare in his veins, a flash of fear so hot he looked to the limerock walls of the Front above him, seeking the safety of grey peaks and cornflower sky. Twin contrails bent west above him, splayed and knotted by wind. He saw the weather was changing, and he realized that the water around his legs had leveled off at his knees.

The bear heaved herself erect and swayed there, damp forepaws treading air, belly fleece matted with the chaff of her travels, ears perked his way. She seemed at once surprised and provoked to find him watching her, but she waited, her eyes hunting over him, her nose working the air. Her pelt hung slack and balding across her paunch, and Horn imagined her waking on the mountain, snuffling about the cavity where she'd wintered, perplexed at the absence of offspring, at waking old and undone to this last season of life.

A second grouse jumped cover and Horn flinched. The bear dropped to all fours and broke into a shuffling rush toward him, snow-brush and willows discharging around her. She came at him head low, her hollowed hindquarters pumping, and Horn thought to lift the spade but did not. The shovel was holding him up.

She slid to a stop just short of the ditch, reared upright again, and rattled her teeth. Horn smelled the sweet fecal musk of bear, and he saw in the black centers of her sunken eyes the horrific force of her life.

"Hey!" Horn said, his voice surprising them both above the murmur of water at his legs. He tucked his chin and tried to brace for what came next.

The bear dropped to her front quarters, sidled back an uncertain step, and grunted low in her throat, a harsh ripple of sound like the amplified tearing of meat. Sidelong she regarded him with one eye, the white-tipped guardhairs on her meager back stiff as quills. In the gap where the soft, inside pink of her lower lip sagged away, Horn saw her broken teeth.

He guessed he could almost touch her muzzle with the spade if he had the heart to lift it, and he realized that what fired the acid through his belly was not just the bear, but also his nightmarish inability to move. The adrenaline scalding through him had once been a friend. Now its burn was only a reminder of the man he had been. For years he had endured its power as the addict survives his drug. Horn knew what it was to be out on his feet and stay on his feet to the end of a round. He took a breath and straightened himself a little. "Come on, old bear," he said, his voice rough and distant in his ears, "just walk away."

At the sound of his voice, she bluffed a charge to the edge of the water and lifted one forepaw to slap him. She waited, flexed and malicious, her monstrous head turned up to him as if expecting a kiss.

Don't you move, Horn told himself, not thinking until later how silly that notion was. He held himself and watched her breathe, until, still humped in threat, she turned and slouched stiffly off, stopping twice to peer over her shoulder before wading the ditch and breaking into a grunting downhill run that took her quickly out of sight.

111

Chickadees slipped through the willows around him. Down the mountain, in the direction the bear had gone, a pine squirrel worked itself into a fit, its frenzied chatter nerving the stillness. Clouds piled over the edge of the Front. The water sucked at Horn's useless legs.

He leaned into the hillside above him until he was on all fours, then kneed his way out of the water and crawled a few feet to a mat of sun-warmed juniper at the base of a fallen tree. He sat against the snag to rest, feeling as if he'd run a long way winded.

Horn listened to the gurgle of water going by, and he listened for sounds of movement in the brush, deciding after several minutes that the bear would not come back. He waited a while longer, then unlaced his sodden boots, pried them off, and wrung out his socks. His hands still shook, and his feet, pale and distant at the ends of his legs, seemed capable only of betrayal. He closed his eyes to slits and listened to rumors of wind on the upper slopes. Wind with weather on it, coming over the mountains from the west.

A woodpecker in the trees behind him tapped soft wood.

Horn felt the last spasms seep away, his terror slowly replaced by exhaustion and sweet relief that nonetheless mingled with a growing premonition of coming trouble, as if the bear had been a sign, a portent of coiled grief or ruin. He opened his eyes and watched two ravens slip and dive, stunting on the wind. The squirrel had stilled; the woods had gone soft and easy again.

He could count the times he'd seen big bears in this country on one hand, yet nothing was ever secure, Horn told himself, no matter how a man safeguarded his life. But that was what had plagued him all winter; that was what he'd been doing these past twelve years, feeding the same sad cows each winter and eating road dust on the county crew every summer while taking a minimum of risks. Twelve years of nights spent alone in a two-room log cabin, twelve years of work and, for release, a few fast rounds on the heavy bag hanging in his barn. A life of rituals without relief, a life without a plan.

Horn looked into the sky, where the first low clouds rushed past, thinking again of the bear. He remembered the electric jolt of fear that had gone right through him like a good punch, and he wondered, *Is that it? Is it the fear I miss?*

He pulled the red skirts of the blanket coat over his thighs, and reminded perhaps by the quality of light angling through the trees, Horn remembered his father leading him by the hand on the radiant fall morning of his first day at school. They passed a row of overhanging elms and a stone wall capped with coarse cement, his father asking did he know how to catch the bus, and satisfied that he did, walking with him past the white kids smirks and the Blackfeet kids' appraising looks toward the double front doors of that terrible place where at six years old he would be left on his own. And Horn was brave that morning because his father was there and his father was brave. Laramie was just a young jack then with his fast eyes and quick hands, a man proud to have a son in school. Laramie was something in those days, someone you could trust. In a flicker of understanding, Horn saw how much he had leaned on his father that morning, and how, in some secret way he could see but not quite say, he had leaned on him ever since.

Horn let his mind turn back to the man who taught him how to box and the Saturday nights and the gloves like pillows, when his father took him to face other boys in country bars. Nights remembered as circles of men in roaring bright saloons who cheered the other kid. Nights of shame and rage, of pain and fright, that went on until Horn compressed his fear. He found speed because he had to, and power, because, to his surprise, it was there. After a dozen good beatings, he stepped in one night and knocked the other kid down. But through a hundred such fights the fear was always there, driving each jab and combination, putting the jolt in each left hook.

Horn spread his socks beside him to dry and settled back against the stump; he clasped his hands, closed his eyes, and inhaled deeply, grateful for the warmth of sun on his face and the fullness of air in his lungs. Thinking of his father, then the bear, then his father again, Horn drifted away toward sleep where dream and memory bled together, drawing him down into the uncertain safety of his past.

He was a boy again, cutting hay. Heat waves rose before him from the tractor's shimmering hood, distorting the blue-green stand of alfalfa and the mountains above him into bands of light. He could taste gasoline from the siphon hose. He could smell hay sap and hot grease. He was by himself in the field.

Wind-turned clouds topped mountains along the Front, and he watched them build as he drowsed to the rattle of pitman shaft and the sizzle of reciprocal knife. He held to a rear fender with one hand and steered with the other, imagining he could see the stand of hay decline with each round, imagining his father praising him for a job well done when he returned from town, imagining his mother, home again. Most clearly, though, he imagined tall glasses of iced water.

The August sky bore down on him with force. He prayed for clouds and fought the urge to sleep by singing songs he'd learned on his mother's radio. He tried Conway Twitty's version of "Only Make-believe," his young voice frogging low notes, then climbing to break on the line, "You are my very soul." He did a couple of teenage car-wreck songs and one of his favorite surfer hits. He rode, sunburned and happy, singing to the precise turning of machinery, singing to himself beneath towers of cloud building toward the sun.

The field seemed to narrow, and he kept on, planning to complete it before anyone returned. He had decided to do this on his own; after all, he was almost a man. If everyone else took off, he'd put up the hay himself. He'd cut it and rake it, bale it and haul the bales home. That's what he was doing alone in the field.

When only a long elliptical swath remained, he stopped, climbed unsteadily down, and with his straw hat, chased two young cottontails and a file of baby grouse from the remaining cover. As he climbed back onto the tractor, he imagined himself sixteen, taking Victoria Pineday to a dance at Augusta in his father's Ford. Victoria Pineday had the best grades in school, and she wore her auburn hair combed forward over each shoulder to hide her brand new breasts.

A raindrop struck his cheek, and as he engaged the clutch, he saw Laramie coming across the mown field, gunning the Ford over slick mounds of hay. The truck came on fast, a few more drops sliced by, and he sensed that what was about to happen, would not be as he'd hoped.

His father got out of the pickup. He was unshaven, and one pearl-buttoned pocket hung torn from his best white shirt. A puffed lip; under one eye, a mouse. He gripped a lug on the rear tractor tire, his careless hand embossed with hard veins and scars; he stared at the field, then at Horn. "What," he said, "are you doing?" his whiskied voice rising to match the wind tossing his hair. "Radio says three days of rain."

Horn switched off the engine. He noticed his younger brother in the truck. Randall, bored by it all, too smart to make a mistake like this.

His father stepped away from the tractor and lit a smoke with trembling hands. He looked at the field and at the cigarette and shook his head.

"Did you find Mom?" Horn asked.

"You cut this all today, didn't you?" his father answered, his voice gone soft, his damp eyes following the first dim sheets of rain drifting off the mountains.

"Dad?" Horn said and woke to find his hands and face wet. Snowflakes the size of nickels fell from a woolen sky, whitening his pants and the juniper boughs around his legs. Horn brushed himself off with his Scotch cap, pulled on his socks, and laced his boots, the down-at-heel loggers wooden on his wet feet. He got up, shook himself, and stood suspended between his dream and the make-believe landscape veiled in storm around him. He saw faces in treeboles under frightwigs of moss, hobgoblins and bogeys of knotholes and sticks. Horn looked full circle, listening to the creak and sigh of the storm. He tipped his head back and caught a snowflake on his tongue. The floating dobs of white seared his uplifted face, tracking down the smile lines around his mouth, and falling in droplets to the exposed vee of his throat. It could have been winter, and, as in his dream, the man a boy again.

Horn laughed at that. He picked up his shovel, jumped the ditch, and set off along the bank path toward home, swinging the spade ahead like a staff and enjoying the apparitions of aspen looming from the storm. He lost his sense of direction as the ditch doubled back in gulches, following the contour of foothills from west to north and around to east, then back to north and west again, going past trees that grew taller the lower he went, until waist-high pitch stumps appeared where the old-time woodhawks had worked.

Horn left the ditch and cut downhill, planning to go on until he found the remnants of rail fence that would guide him quickly home. He let the grade pull him into a trot and went along in zig-zags through clots of limber pine, boot heels and spade kicking up splotches of duff, wind whistling in his throat. On flatter ground he ran, his long legs light and quick, bursts of breath fogging his wake. He strained to see, feeling giddy and young as he picked up speed. His breath came harder, and his sense of lightness increased until he felt like laughing again.

But the fence he found was half a mile from the one he wanted, and he did not laugh as he slowed to a stop at the rectangle of wire around a stand of trees the woodcutters had left. He leaned on the gate at the entrance until he caught his wind, then opened it and went into the place where the *Métis* lay buried under stones bearing their names. Parenteau, he read. Lepine, Otter, Dumont. Charpentier, Lamere, Fleury, Horn. A row of Horns, the old ones overgrown with wild rose, the rest overgrown with grass. Room for more.

He bent and swept snow from a toppled stone and read the name he'd heard so often as a child, the name of the woman who helped the others to Montana after the Rebellion up north was lost. When Horn was a boy, those who remembered her were children when she died, and now it was possible that he alone remembered what they'd said. This much, in weathered script, was left:

MARGUERITE HORN
Saint Vital, Manitoba, 1806
South Pass, Montana, 1894
MATRIARCH

Horn shuddered and realized that his coat was soaked clear through. He put his hands into his pockets and looked at the row of bloods that included his uncles—men he could remember, if only dimly—his father's older brothers. And there at the end of the line, under the root-bound sod like all the rest, lay his father.

Horn turned away and saw, on an uncommonly large aspen that grew in a sunken, unmarked trough in the ground, a carved heart, bisected by a crude arrow shot between two sets of initials. And he saw how the bark had scarred black where he'd stripped it once to green. He had been green himself that summer, and Victoria a year younger. They had not just gone to dances. They had come here, to this sheltered spot in the woods. Horn felt an unexpected sweetness pass through him as he looked at this holy place where he had learned to love.

He closed the gate, made the sign of the cross, and ran on, following elk trails through the trees.

In a bowl where hillside clay once sloughed and folded to a stop, Horn passed a hot springs pool, celadon and deep. Then Mad Laurent's woodcamp with its tin can dump and rust-gutted stove, a set of bobsled runners and cap-sized bolsters hidden by needles and duff.

Lower on the mountain and nearly free of the timber, he crossed her tracks, padding off into the gloom—an old bear wandering alone in the storm, trudging down the mountain through Garland Pineday's upper pasture. Horn cut west off her track and went on, wanting to check the dams he'd set that morning, anxious to see the stain of water spreading out across his land.

He was almost to open ground and still running, phrases of Twitty's long-ago song echoing like fragments of dream in his mind, when it came to him to wonder—as he might have wondered once as a boy—why the dreams came at all. Had it been dreams and days of childhood that brought him back to a home where so much had been lost? Was it dreams that held him there, at times against his will? Or, had he taken, he wondered, too many shots to the head?

What he wanted, Horn thought, was really not so hard. Just a chance to leave for a while, to take off up north and see some country with folding money in his pocket to unfold and spend. Or south, on the Norton he'd kept all this time in a shed. He'd explain it to Victoria. She'd know what to do.

He vaulted the jackfence at the edge of the timber and crossed a swale overgrown with balsamroot and sage, land he owned in uneasy common trust with the Great Falls lawyer who was his brother.

He crossed the snowline midway down the last bald ridge above his fields and slowed to a walk in misting rain, buoyed to be off the mountain, to be out in the open again.

Horn stopped to catch his wind and ease the ache in his side. He bent to rest, gripping his knees with his hands, and when he lifted his head to flex his neck, he saw a slim white line of smoke rising from the stovepipe at the front of his shack. "Ah, girl," he said. And gladness ran through him and warmed him.

From where he stood, most of the cabin was hidden by lilacs that grew to its eaves, but in the rain the corrugated tin roof seemed luminous, as if lit from within. Just beyond the cabin, at the edge of a draw wooded with doghair fir, an unpainted frame house stood open to weather, home only to mice and wood rats and flies. It had been an improvement no one could endure, that house of calamity built by his father, where, during Horn's early manhood, his family had come apart. Below the house, partly hidden by a grove of waning cottonwoods, Horn could see the dormered mow of his log barn and the west end, too, of the pole corrals and sorting pens.

He looked back at his cabin and watched the smoke twist up through pelting rain to pierce the lowering sky. The rain blued the air around him, smudging the first dim greens of grasslands and meadows to muted shades of lifeless grey. Below him, the ditch from Blanchard Creek entered a box made of concrete and stone. The water plunged in, dropped a foot, and surged through headgates left and right to smaller ditches contouring the upper lengths of the field. Down each ditch Horn could see the plastic dams he'd set that morning, bellied tight but holding. Water, backed by the dams, spilled over ditch banks and slowed to a sheen as it soaked level ground. Above the continuing white sound of rain came the concord of water in motion, undulant and gentle, polyphonic and clear.

A pair of mallards veered from their course along the tule bottoms to inspect Horn's dams. They quacked past craning their necks, and Horn quacked back. He wiped his face with his hands, and rubbed his hands on his jeans, feeling foolish and full of life, a grown man uplifted by the physical forces of the world around him. He was wet clear through and growing cold, but he lingered a few moments, letting his anticipation build and listening to the rain accelerate as the light began to fail.

He lifted his face and closed his eyes and let the rain pound his skin. In darkness and rain and lost time he glimpsed again how good that searing spring had been, and he saw how the heat he'd found for a girl, when he was not much more than a boy, was reborn in the way he'd come to feel about her, now that he was a man.

Victoria had grown up too, and her flaming hair had darkened with time almost to black. After college in Bozeman, where she graduated a structural engineer, she hit the tank town refineries to ride out the boom. From Wyoming she went overseas, and the jobs in the desert kept her away a year or two at a stretch. When Horn quit fighting and came home to stay, she had been gone long enough. He settled in, saw other women when he could, almost talked himself into marriage once. When he least expected it, she would simply reappear.

The last time she'd come home, Horn had driven into his yard after eight numbing hours in a dump truck to find her perched loose-limbed with a tumbler of bourbon in the golden willow out front. He parked the pickup as usual, took his lunch box from the seat, and, as he walked toward her, dusted his jeans with his baseball cap. Victoria watched without expression, waiting for his dust to settle before she broke his heart.

Horn slowed in the uncut grass, squinting up into the spangled light of sun and leaves, a hard guy taking his time. He looked from her scuffed boots to the jeans worn thin at knee and thigh, then paused with intent on the chambray shirt, unbuttoned to the tops of her freckled breasts. Then the flash of teeth and chestnut skin, her cat's eyes, otter brown—a smile quick and certain, ending with a careless toss of her head.

In her husky voice she asked, "And how's my handsome lad?"

Horn remembered how he'd cleared his throat and swayed inside. He had tried for words. "I'm glad to see you." That's what he said.

The ducks swung back, making a lower pass, and Horn remembered the aspen in the cemetery that bore their initials, a tree well-nourished as it grew through the bones of some lost and nameless soul.

At a hundred yards he saw her coming toward him through the dusk, wearing an oilskin slicker and what looked like one of his broken Stetson hats. She carried a bottle by its neck in her gloved right hand and walked looking down, the rain sluicing past her front from the hat's sodden felt.

Horn stepped through the new grass and mud feeling the life inside him rise. In that person he saw the course of his past, and in that person he discovered again a cause for hope. He opened his mouth to call her name, skidded in the cowpath muck, and glanced down. When he looked up, he saw Garland Pineday standing there instead.

"Garland?" Horn said, and in one stride he saw how it could all go wrong.

Pineday stood rigid as a post. He hadn't shaved in a couple of days, and his whiskered chin was white. He did not look drunk, yet he was not the kind of man to fire your stove while you were gone. He handed the bottle of Dickel over, Horn took it and held it to his chest.

"You're cold," Pineday said.

"It's bad?" Horn answered.

Pineday looked past him up the meadows, a small man of almost delicate build, known in that country as a trainer of horses. He cut his eyes back to Horn. "You drink some of that," he said in the voice he used when working colts, "and we'll go on up to the house."

Horn fumbled the cap away and put the bottle to his lips. He drank, then drank again, the whiskey running from his chin as he began to shake. Without speaking again they faced about and walked through the drifting veils of rain toward the sourceless blue light of the shack's tin roof and the hanging fronds of the willow out front, where nothing would ever be new again.

Big Sky Journal 1995

At the Edge of Things
From *Lady*, a novel in progress

He stands in wind and morning light, watching clay-bank tablelands to the north, where wheat-farmed dirt rides warming air. He wears work clothes, even on this most festive day, a dun Resistol stained along the band, jeans pale with age, broken Wesco loggers and a denim shirt, the cuffs twice-folded, exposing walnut forearms that reach to hands hard-veined and scarred. He leans against the bone-white handles of a walking plow cantilevered toward the county road, transom for a mailbox bearing in faded letters the name Countryman.

At his back a shelterbelt: six horseshoe-shaped rows of stricken spruce and olive that enclose an orchard and the buildings hidden within. Among the trees a pheasant bells. Blackbirds come from cattail sloughs, winging toward the weed-bound farmland he faces, their shadows lancing his like so many missiles. Across the road, a sign nailed to a sawhorse reads:

FARM SALE!
Free Lunch

Dust rises above the section road to the west, and beneath it, bunched as if for protection, a ragged column of trucks and pickups, a few pulling fifth-wheel trailers, others trailing phantoms of boom and bust. They come in rattletrap sedans and third-hand flatbeds, vehicles distorted into rubbery motion by corduroyed road and heat as they top the last hill, a column of neighbors and other unfortunates—or a parade of the crazed, who can tell?—come all this way to feed at auction.

They slow, downshifting to make the turn, some drivers nodding or giving two-fingered salutes from steering wheels to the man at the plow, who dips his chin in return—bland acknowledgment of one to another, each and all children of this place, their necks cracked like mud flats by the same sun, pale eyes hardened by the same hard miles of loss. No two among them friends.

Stragglers arrive alone or in pairs. A fox crosses, as if directed by a traffic signal. The aluminum lunch wagon passes, high school girls aflame in its windows, yearning for escape. A Dodge diesel turns in, followed by a Blazer with star decals on doors and hood, which stops, backs, and stops again beside the plow with a metallic pong of transmission jammed into PARK. The driver's tinted window comes down an inch, two, then the rest of the way, followed by a cool wash of air from within as the deputy leans out to spit.

The pearled Stetson shades a nose gone to bloodshot mush from youthful violence and latter-day drink. Hard fat over muscle packed into a shirt a size too small. Leopard's eyes. In a voice almost resigned: "Horn, you going to be your natural self and give me some grief here today?"

The man so addressed slides burled hands into hip pockets, leans down. "You'll sure be the first to know, Bob."

The deputy coughs a faint snort far back in the clogged passages of his ruined nose. "Sure," he says with a twist of his head that brings them eye to eye, one tribe of hunter facing another. Then he sighs, taps the steering wheel with his wedding ring, drops the Blazer into gear with a meaty hand, and pulls languidly away as the two men exchange wolfy grins.

Lastly a boy treadles past on a bicycle, sweating, thin legs in jeans tied about at the ankles with twine to keep his cuffs from the chain. It is a girl's Schwinn, balloon tires nearly bald, yet the boy dismounts beyond the mailbox as if from a roping horse sitting back on a calf. A sunny boy from a jelly jar label, scion of the failed come out from town, where he summers with his dead folks' kin. He looks at Horn, almost stops, then continues down the weeded lane toward the amplified shrieks of a PA system gone wrong. Horn knows the boy, was present the day he was named and blessed.

In the dirt yard between house and sheds, a rude platform has been cobbled from plywood and two-by-fours atop an iron-wheeled hay wagon. Beyond it, stretching to either side and backed by the westerly run of shelter belt, stands a row of tractors, trucks, and implements, which men climb upon or kick with impunity. Off to one side, an almost new Gleaner combine. And for antiques, a galvanized threshing machine with wooden spouts; a sulky plow and middle buster with fenestrated iron seats; a fanning mill, half-filled by the nightly labors of trade rats with bolts and bones and sticks. Directly beneath the auctioneer's dais, two zinc-covered milkhouse tables, littered with household items, hand tools, a half-dozen rifles, and assorted tack draw those in need of gossip and a chance to bid, if bids stay small.

With bear-like quickness the auctioneer heaves himself onto the platform, where a young woman gazes beyond the rows of hats and caps at God knows what as she waits with a grinding of teeth for the sale to begin. The pitchman waves a bullprick cane, holds a microphone to burgundy lips. "Boys," he says, puffing his cheeks and cocking his head as if to listen, "she don't get much better than this. The machinery has all been shedded, the vehicles got one name only on the pink slips. The buildings are sound, and the land speaks for itself. All this place needs is a good woman, some kids, and a little sweat to bring 'er around. Hell, you know that."

He takes off his lid, mops his face with a rag, sets the hat down low again over pinpoint eyes. "It's gonna get hot up here," he says with a cheesy grin, "so let's get her sold. Item number one: A 1970 Ford, ton-and-a-half truck with eighteen-foot bed, grain box, and hoist—be just the ticket for a spare during harvest. I need fifteen hundred to get us started. Fifteen, gimme fifteen, five . . ." The roundness of his voice grows richer, spreading in volume to encompass those listening and those gazing blankly about. A voice full of promise that half those assembled there recognize as the self-same venal pronouncement of greed that whispers to them of their most secret lust, which is the need to claim, to grasp, to own.

Yet only two men, neighbors and cousins at that, show interest. They stand shoulder to shoulder, bidding the truck back up from the auctioneer's vexed low to sell at nine hundred dollars.

"Friends," from this hawker in country garb, "let's don't be this way. If we can't sell it here, we can darn sure sell it down the road. What we are not going to do is give it away. Now wake up and come on!" He aims the varnished bull pizzle at an International 2+2 articulated tractor with duals all the way around, three remotes, cab air, AM/FM/cassette. "Look at those tires. Just been majored, too. There's a hundred and seventy horses ready to go to work, so give me thirty thousand for her and drive 'er home." Again the chanting of amplified numbers spills over the uplifted faces where flies circle and settle at will.

After a while the fat man stops counting backwards and sighs. "Boys . . ." he says, his marbled voice trailing off as a man in a white straw hat and short-sleeved shirt steps onto the rostrum beside him. He takes the auctioneer's paw in his own, swings microphone and hand as one to his mouth, says, "Neighbors, I know these folks were well-liked around here. Nobody's forcing them to sell. They just want out. You sure can't help them by treating an honest sale this way, so let's get this over or go home." He releases the auctioneer's hand and takes one step back, clearing the fat man's line of sight, yet keeping his eyes moving from one to another of the men standing below, knowing that among those who recognize him there are some who hold his service in low regard. But how many times has he held paper for Dutch? Or sold ground for guys like Archie? Or helped others like Dale turn a 1031? His eyes stop for a moment on each of them until he comes to a man off by himself, a dark man, one hand tucked to the thumb in his pants above the zipper, the other hanging loose at his side. *Some blood there*, the Broker thinks, *down from the reservation, looking for work or something to steal.*

The auctioneer's voice gains momentum, tongue and jaw ratcheting numbers until someone in the second row waves and the bidding begins. The International sells for nine thousand and change.

Smaller tractors, tumblebug plows, chisel bottoms with rod-weeders; discs, drills, harrows, and the old thresher sell in slow succession, then a Powder River chute with some pipe panels, bundles of fence posts, irrigation pipe, a drill press, welder and torch. No one bids on the combine, though several go after an assortment of bolts and nails in buckets, then two mounds of bent and rust-pitted scrap iron.

Of the items on the milkhouse tables, saddles and harness sell first, the harness still oiled, the saddles ready for use. A .250-3000 Savage goes for a hundred dollars less than pawnshop price. A Model 72 Winchester .22 comes up, and the Broker steps forward again, says he'd like to bid on the rifle if nobody minds. "Had one just like it on my daddy's place."

The barker faces around, spreads his left hand as if to sell the Broker himself. "Twenty-five bucks," he says. The Broker nods, smiling the smile of a deal already done.

"Thirty," from somewhere in the crowd.

The Broker shrugs, nods, looks to the auctioneer, who takes a bid of forty, grins with ill-disguised ennui, and twirls his index finger in an upward gyre.

Fifty, sixty, seventy, the price climbs a brief thermal of enthusiasm until the frivolous fold their arms, and those who have shilled the price for fun shake their heads. At a hundred and sixty dollars only the breed stays in, squatting on his boot heels, scratching dirt with a stick, which he lifts to mark his bid when the auctioneer barks and points his way.

Heads turn back and forth with sly and furtive glances. Elbows find neighbors' ribs. The deputy, corndog in hand, wipes mustard from the corner of his mouth. At two hundred and thirty dollars the auctioneer goes silent, looks at the man beside him, who is no longer having fun. The Broker wonders if the buck is drunk, then shakes his head, says, "Nope. Too rich for me."

When nothing remains but dirt, they sell that: four sections of cropland, 320 acres of coulee bottom pasture, and the quarter where the buildings stand. A man wearing baggy shorts buys the whole works. The auctioneer gives half-hearted thanks to those few left, and, bending to check the bookkeeper's figures, says, "Aw, shit."

"Well, shit yourself, John," the woman answers, fanning herself with a sale flier with one hand while writing a receipt for a jug-eared farmer with watery eyes, who turns away in scarlet confusion.

"I'll be wanting my check," the auctioneer tells the Broker.

"Soon as we get ours, you get yours."

Horn yawns, looks from those departing to the orchard and swale of coulee, where he and Mace Countryman shot gophers, spring evenings after school. Mace was about as fair as a kid could get, but they had nonetheless been school bus buddies. Later, friends.

Horn lays cash for the .22 before the auctioneer's assistant, neglects the federal firearms form, and is lifting the rifle from the table when he becomes aware of someone at his shoulder. Horn extracts the tubular magazine, opens the bolt, closes it, tries the safety, which holds. He reopens the action. He remembers the ivory bead on the end of the barrel exactly, and the Redfield peep, too, mounted atop the breech. Where tang met stock, the initials M C lay carved in the oiled wood. He looks at the man in the white straw hat and short-sleeved shirt—held together at the throat with a bolo of turquoise the size of a coyote turd—as he slides the empty magazine home.

Horn lifts his eyebrows.

"That popgun mean something special to you, Chief?"

"Yes, sir, it does," Horn says, feeling the muscles at the backs of his arms go goosey, as if straining toward speed. The broker cuts him a look, then waves and calls to someone off to the side.

As Horn walks toward his El Camino he nods to an officer of the law who leans among the tansy against the cold steel of a Butler bin, taking his ease with glugmug in hand, near the end of his shift. Old Bob nods back and winks.

A couple miles down the road Horn catches up with the boy pushing his bicycle.

"Hey," Horn says, slowing to a stop beside him.

The kid looks at him, doesn't have anything to say.

"This was your daddy's," Horn says, lifting the rifle through the window and holding it, barrel up, by its pistol grip. The boy doesn't move. Wind touches his wheatstraw hair.

"Come on, take it. It's yours now."

The boy reaches, touches the rifle, lifts it awkwardly by the harness leather sling.

"Anybody says anything, you tell them to call Clayton, over on Blanchard Creek. They'll know."

With that Horn pulls the Hurst into low and idles away, listening to the uneven roll of crank and cam as he accelerates over a rise, not daring to look in the mirror until it's too late to see the son of a friend lost at just this time of year, in hills not so very much unlike these, a lad standing alone and open-faced at the edge of the road in some weeds.

Big Sky Journal 1999

THE HARDER THEY COME

When he hit the second wind-slabbed drift on Cutler Grade, Gregor MacIvers knew he wouldn't make it home that night without his chains. A spume of fine snow lofted from the hood and misted his windshield, and as the engine stalled, the truck shuddered to a stop. Spindrift sluiced off the plow berm at the west edge of the road, rising in tight vortices beyond the reach of his lights. And for an instant in the swirling space at the edge of darkness, MacIvers saw or imagined a woman standing in a light summer dress, her coiling black hair tracing the currents of wind behind her. He started his engine and rubbed the windshield with the flat of his hand; even with the lights switched to high beam, he saw nothing ahead but a ground-blizzard at night.

MacIvers backed a few yards down his tracks, and watched as grooves cut by his truck's undercarriage began again to fill with snow. He snapped on the dome light and reached for his insulated coveralls. He'd known all day he would have to feed when he got home, yet he had lingered in town over a solitary dinner, celebrating again, as he had for the past four Friday nights, the torment of his divorce. It was an expensive ritual that seemed to do him no good.

As he opened his door and began to step out, MacIvers saw in the confusion of tools and winter clothes crowding the bright cab, that he'd forgotten his felt-lined winter overshoes. He wiggled his toes in the hand-tooled Mexican riding boots he wore and said without heat, "Real pretty."

Stars appeared beyond torn clouds as he zipped the coveralls over his herringbone sports jacket, an extravagance he'd allowed himself a month before on the day he appeared in court. The coat had seemed a good idea at the time, an excusable self-indulgence, a last minute defense against town and what waited there beyond his control. Now it was only a coat, and not very warm at that.

MacIvers ran the coverall zippers down his legs, pulled on a wool Scotch cap, and plowed around to the toolbox in the back. He moved fast, knowing his feet would suffer. In wind that cut through any cloth made, MacIvers wrestled his chains into place on the lugged tires. He crawled under the truck behind each wheel and fastened the first three inside hooks without trouble. As he struggled for slack on the last one, he wondered if he'd set the emergency brake. A premonition of the truck rolling back drove him to squirm out and check. The brake handle was pulled all the way up; that he couldn't remember touching it, gave MacIvers a moment's pause. Sometimes in the past few weeks he would set off on an errand to one of his outbuildings and on the way forget what he'd meant to do. That could be dangerous when a man worked alone. It was the little mistakes, MacIvers knew, that got you in trouble.

He forced each V-bar cross-chain around the tire, straining slack toward the inside hook. Snow, packed in the channel iron frame above him, melted under the heat of the idling engine and dripped on his neck. "We're having fun now," he grunted, gripping the length of sidechain with both bare hands and feeling the links bite his calloused fingers as he applied his strength. After he fastened the hook, he lay on his side a moment to rest, his face relaxed in the endearing chill of snow.

Headlights swept the grade below as he finished, the snapping of chains on fenders rising to him on the wind. He slammed the toolbox closed, cursed his numb feet, and stepped back as a new Dodge flatbed, loaded with a couple tons of cattle cake, eased to a stop beside his truck. Melvin Rathbone rolled down his window and showed his teeth. He was wearing a Swiss alpine hat with feathers.

Melvin and his older brother, Junior, lived on a remnant of their long-dead parent's heartbreak homestead which they hadn't yet subdivided, like the rest of their place, for summer homes. In their eighties, both Rathbones stood less than five feet tall, and their teeth, which hadn't seen a dentist since the Great War, made even MacIvers wince.

"Told you he was stuck," Melvin said, looking MacIvers right in the face.

Brother Junior stared ahead under the loop of steering wheel at snow purling through his lights. "Wouldn't be if we had our new road. Screw him."

Melvin knotted his wrinkled little face like a wizened fist. "Hard guy, yeah. But," he decided, his hooded eyes hot slits in the corrugated ruin of his face, "you're alone now."

"I was 'til you come along," MacIvers said. "You get moving, I'll take my lonesomeness home and warm it up."

"She's not coming back, Gregor," Melvin nickered. He waved as the Dodge churned ahead, gaping back for an instant like an evil dwarf in a child's fevered dream. MacIvers climbed into his truck, held his hands above the defroster and waited until the funnel of receding light ahead disappeared beyond the crest above him. Without spinning a wheel, he eased into the fresh tracks, shifted to second gear, and drove steadily on to his first gate, an elaborate structure he'd built in idle hours from scrap iron. He groped for his keys, watching snow swirl through rusted filigree around what he'd meant to be Pegasus in flight. But in the headlights, the iron figure he'd hammered from boiler plate with a cold chisel looked instead like a winged goat.

MacIvers knew how his neighbors felt about his refusal to let the County cross his place with a better road. And although he still thought he'd been right, he understood how that singular choice of land over people had isolated him for good. Maybe that had advantages, he reflected, with neighbors like his.

He closed the gate behind his truck and held the padlock for a moment in his heavy hand, then pitched it into the dark and replaced it with one of several he'd bought that day after paying off his lawyer. Not that he disagreed with Melvin and thought she might come back. No, it was only a way of reminding himself that she couldn't.

A stranger in that country would not have made the next mile, but by leaving his summer road below and following sagebrush ridges swept bare by the wind, MacIvers kept his truck moving toward home. He was now on his own land, land which in the past decade had burdened him with debt, greyed his hair early, worn him out. Four square miles of sidehill grassland, it was still as wild and untouched as the day he bought it, unchanged, probably, since the day Lewis and Clark had passed on their way to the Pacific.

Three months after his father died, MacIvers had gambled on this pasture, and until now, with the added expense of divorce, he'd gained so steadily on the balance that he could almost see an end to it. Land values around him had soared, but years of debt made him cautious; land lasted, and man's mark upon it, long after the man was gone. His father's death had taught him that, and right or wrong, MacIvers knew there would be no roads here until his own death paved their way.

The wind dropped as he entered a pine woods, and he drove on in sudden quiet to his second gate, a massive pole affair topped by a burled yellow pine log, which had marked the former boundary of the ranch. An ox yoke hung on tug chains from the knotted header, and on the yoke, facing what had then been the outside world, MacIver's great-grandfather had seared his name, one flaming letter at a time, with a red-hot length of angle iron.

He changed this lock too, and as he snapped the new one closed MacIvers felt again a wary sense of misgiving—one which he'd lately kept at bay with relentless labor and whiskey. He was alone as he'd never been, completely, and so it seemed, by choice. Voiceless days and nights, welcome at first after the final days his wife had spent in the house, had soon begun to wear on his nerves. And as he looked at the lock and chain, he knew this would be his answer, his reply to her and the life she wanted. What bore his name he intended to keep untouched, no matter what the price in silence or cash.

He made water in the dark beside the gate and noticed that the wind had completely stopped. To the west, the sky was salted with stars, yet in the absence of wind the night seemed even colder. He would change clothes at the house and build a fire in the range before going to the barns. The kitchen would be warm when he returned, and he could re-map his life with bourbon at the lamplit table in peace.

MacIvers fiddled with the radio as he drove on, picking up a rock station in Bozeman, the Country FM in Helena, then classical music from Butte. He made a practice of playing the radio whenever he worked around cattle in the dark, imagining they were calmed by music. He turned up the volume, found the bottle under his seat, and while holding the first hot slash of whiskey tight against his lips, tried to guess Monteverdi or Scarlatti. With the satisfying burn of Walker's came too the vague but familiar pride of having once again made it home on a bad night.

Fighting roads was something of a family tradition—dozens of nights, dimmed now by time and run together in memory, young MacIvers had waited at the highway with a team of Percheron horses to pull his parents' car the rest of the way home. That urge toward home on a hard night was something he had wanted to pass on. His eyes watered as MacIvers drank again. "To us," he said in mock-toast to his image in the windshield, "the dead and the stillborn." The music, he realized, was Henry Purcell's, and he put the bottle away.

Yet his eyes still teared as he drove past the house and down the long hill to the barns. When he caught his mistake, he stopped the truck and hardened his mouth. He would have to put his mind on one thing at a time until his work was done. It could wander all it wanted later, in the lamplight. Hereford cattle, their iridescent eyes turned blindly toward him, milled in the truck lights, smoky breath rising over their frosted backs. Beyond them stood the haybarn, massive, cribbed high along the outside with corral rails, and filled to the rafters with sweet alfalfa hay. From the air, the three barns together looked like a giant galvanized T, the haybarn and adjoining log cowbarn intersected midway by a long tin feedshed. MacIvers knew it would be dry in the haybarn and in the plank-floored feed manger next door. He wouldn't have to worry about his feet if he hustled, and then, he thought, he'd be through for the night. The idea of feeding cattle in the herringbone jacket brought a smile; he turned off the lights and engine, letting the radio play on in the dark.

MacIvers climbed a ladder to the first level, then another, up to the very top of the stack, some twenty-five feet above the feedshed door. From there he dragged one bale at a time with a long-handled hook to the edge of the stack, and by the strings, pitched them out into the darkness below. He needed fifty, which he would then pull into the plank-floored feed bunk and break for the cows. The lack of light didn't matter; his eyes gradually adjusted, and besides, he knew the place by heart.

The musty smell of dry alfalfa reminded him, as it often did, of his father, a silent, patient man remembered for his ability with animals. It was said that MacIvers' father could gentle anything with hair; that when you brought him a colt, you'd take home a horse. The haybarn had been their last shared labor, one which brought them together at the time of his father's failing health, when, during the dangers of working at such heights, they had wordlessly exchanged the roles of father and son.

After he dropped thirty bales, MacIvers stopped to rest. Though his body seemed warm in the padded coveralls, his feet were wooden again, and his face, which had been badly frostbitten several times, burned with a dull ache. I should have stopped at the house first, he thought and slapped his gloved hands together.

High in the hayshed rafters, where they joined the log barn his grandfather had built, MacIvers noticed his cat coming toward him along a beam. The man made a sound with his lips; the cat paused then came on. A peculiar animal, he didn't meow or purr or mingle with the other cats. Except for MacIvers and mice, he left other living things alone. But when MacIvers worked at the barns, the cat followed him like a shadow.

He began to drag bales again, heaving each one with a grunt toward the feedshed door below. As he walked back and forth across the slick hay, his mind turned to another winter night nearly a dozen years before, when, for thirty dollars and a bottle of Walker's, he'd taken a group of college students for a hayride with his father's last team. Among them was a slender girl who had come alone. Before the end of the first mile she moved up to the seat beside him to watch the heavy horses pull in the moonlight. And as the hayboat cut the brittle night, MacIvers discovered a feeling he would later attach to expanses of undisturbed land.

He stopped, realizing he'd lost count. His face had numbed, and even his legs were chilled. "Close enough?" he asked the cat, who watched from a jackbrace overhead. The cat made no sound. "Right you are, Caliban," MacIvers said and started back along the edge toward the uppermost ladder. He felt his outside boot skid on a loose bale, felt the hemp strings, rotted through by mildew or chewed thin by mice, snap under his weight. MacIvers made an off-balance stab at a cross-brace with his hook, missed, and tipped headlong into the cavity between cribbing and stack. He heard his voice as he fell and what sounded like a rifle fired into his neck when he hit. And as the vertical column of his weight bore down upon his burning face, Gregor MacIvers discovered that he could not move.

He opened his eyes. The left side of his face lay flush against the frozen ground, so flat he knew the shoulder beneath him must be smashed. By rolling his eyes, he could see his legs above him, resting against all logic between an upright post and the wall of hay. He could also see through the rail fence in front of him a small portion of meadow and piece of sky. MacIvers knew he'd fallen over thirty feet but guessed he'd been slowed some by the stack and barrier of poles. Perhaps he'd only lost his wind, broken an arm or collarbone, and jarred loose some teeth; that was nothing new. It was the noise in his neck when he landed that frightened him.

The thing to do was relax, right himself as carefully as he could, and get to the house, even if he had to crawl, before he froze his feet. But he couldn't feel his feet. Or his legs. He wasn't really sure where his right arm might be, although his left one seemed to lie somewhere under him. Just catch your wind, he told himself. Take a deep breath and keep thinking. What happened to the hook? But the weight of muscle and bone and gut above him made breathing hard, and he knew he'd have to move soon or suffocate like a bull caught on its back. He strained to bend his legs and nothing moved; a sound in front of his face startled him: the long vowel A. He was shamed by the noise, and he quieted.

Most of the cattle had gone to the far side of the stack, expecting to be fed there as usual. A few, confused by the delay, began to wander back, bawling occasional plumes of smoke. Above the squeal of their hooves on the frozen snow, MacIvers could hear the radio in his truck. A yearling heifer found him, and stretching her neck, peered through the rails at his upturned face. She shook her head and snorted, and he could smell the rich stench of her cud. Above the bulk of the animal, he noticed a few dull stars. It will get colder, he thought, and remembering the cold which he no longer felt, brought MacIvers back to life. Try one thing at a time, man. Find your right hand and wiggle your fingers. At least try. Again he strained in the darkness but found nothing, felt nothing but his own great weight bearing down upon him.

MacIvers worked at breathing. From the angle at which he lay, he studied the roof above him, some rafter ends, the roughcut fir beam they rested on, and a crossbrace rising from post to beam. They had cut the trees during a hard winter, and in the gentle evenings of that wet spring, he and his father had milled the logs into lumber. Working together, they hauled the green, thirty-foot rafters from the mill and ricked them like a charcoal pyre where the barn now stood. That autumn they raised the lodgepole posts and with block and tackle lifted the lintels into place. Every hour of spare time they had, they worked on the barn, through the fall and early winter, sheathing the rafters with pine boards, then nailing down bright sheets of tin. MacIvers remembered the hope which had filled him then, as joining the old barn, their luminous structure rose like a landmark of endurance.

The cattle had begun to bed, as if they'd given up on their feed and forgotten MacIvers, who for some time had been unconscious. He held his breath when he woke, catching the melody of a Handel Sarabande. MacIvers tried to smile, although he was no longer sure what he did with his mouth resembled irony. By moving his tongue, he could feel the sharp edges of a broken tooth toward the back of his jaw. He searched for fragments, worrying what might have been a crown toward his lips to spit it out. That's it, he told himself, just hang in there. You've stood frostbite before. Stay calm and try to keep awake. Someone might come.

But MacIvers knew better than that. After the calamity of his wife's second miscarriage, their neighbors and friends gradually stopped dropping by, soured perhaps by MacIver's increasing obsession with work, discouraged by his obvious desire for privacy, his preoccupation with boundaries. And yet, he saw, as he'd isolated himself in work, a distance had grown between him and his work, between him and his land, between him and himself. It hadn't been the County's planned road, MacIvers realized, but a distance he'd created that so finally set him apart.

He felt the sweet dullness creeping over him again and drew as much of the sharp air as he could into his lungs, forcing his mind to range, if not toward escape then at least for a moment of memory he could grasp to pull himself awake. He went back, he thought to the beginning of the trouble, when his father had opposed the marriage—not, MacIvers knew, because the old man hadn't liked Margaret, but because, as he'd said, it would be better to wait. Thinking of that time, MacIvers guessed his father had wanted him to wait on himself, until he had time to season sound enough to stand disappointments like the ones that followed. And he had waited for nearly two years, working longer days, buying and selling cattle with a vengeful cunning that made him respected by older men, and raging continually within himself at the courtship that dragged on, and at the very work which he took more and more upon himself. He lost his sense of humor, and any feeling for fun. During those two years he grew hard; fast to anger, he abused his body as he sometimes abused horses and machines. He became hard on everything and everyone around him, and most of all, he was hard on himself.

Six weeks before the day set for their wedding, MacIvers found his father, sitting as if asleep in the sunny south door of the log barn, facing the vast hay-shed which waited for the first time to be filled. He'd sat down to rest not fifty feet from where MacIvers now lay and died with no sign of pain upon his face. As if sharing his rest, MacIvers sat down beside him in the dovetailed shadows and thought about harvesting alone.

After that, he began to ease up. In his thirties his hair had turned the color of new iron while his body toughened like green wood. He planned his work carefully, hired good help and treated his help well, pacing himself and the hired men with long but gradual days. He might have been happy then except for a vague and abiding regret over the two fevered years he'd ruined. Children, a son especially, he believed would have eased him, but even that had been beyond his power. When the second child died inside his wife, their life together began to die too. She withdrew into a world of magazines, television, and cigarettes at the house, and MacIvers abandoned her for his woods and fields. In the evenings he engrossed himself in books, music, and a growing lust for more land. He put money they couldn't spare on the Hammerstorm place to the south and spent most of his time there building new fences. It was then that men like the Rathbones, who were old enough to remember, began to compare MacIvers with his great grandfather, and although it was often with anger when they spoke of "that overreaching old son of a bitch," MacIvers was drawn, almost in spite of himself, to emulate a man he'd never known.

"This is one way to get it done," he said, his voice rising from habit. "You just get down here like this, beside each post, and check its alignment with the rest." Margaret seemed doubtful; she stood just beyond the cribbing in a summer dress, holding her elbows cupped in her hands, cradling her breasts. "I don't see what difference it makes now, Mac," she said.

"I don't guess you would," he answered, watching the wind lace her raven hair into veils across her face.

"I'm sorry about the whole deal," she said.

"Maybe we ought to give it another try," and MacIvers was about to say he was sorry too, when Melvin Rathbone lurched up on stumpy legs and clicked his amber teeth. "No!" Melvin said. "You changed your locks!"

"Maggie?" MacIvers said, coming awake enough to notice his cat walking a rail above him. The animal brushed his leg. Arching its back it turned and seemed to touch him again. MacIvers pursed his lips, then thought better of it. He wished he had stopped to change his clothes like he'd planned, wished he could stay awake, even wished for a drink.

Glancing between the rails toward the dark house, MacIvers was startled to see lights coming through the trees beyond the pole gate. Someone, for a reason he couldn't begin to guess, was driving down his lane. He blinked to make certain it wasn't still a dream, then thought, kids—drinking and cruising around. Likely they'd found the maze of development roads at Rathbone's, got lost, and cut his fence. But if they stopped at the gate, they might hear his radio.

Although he couldn't open his mouth, he knew he could make sound. He drew and held a deep breath, straining to hear the approaching vehicle and telling himself to wait a little longer before making his shameful noise. But as he strained his aching eyes, the light left the road, climbing into the dry lower limbs of trees beyond the gate where no road ran. And with absolute clarity MacIvers saw the terrible joke of his life; he released the air he'd held and gasped for more to laugh at the moon, rising as it would for eternity, upon his land.

The Last Best Place 1988

BIG SPENDERS

Teenagers rode ropes from cliffs above a summer pond. At the final rising instant they kicked free and fell, windmilling their arms through leaf-dappled light. A boy and girl in cutoffs plunged hand in hand toward the glassy surface of water; laughing as they fell, they let go of each other the moment they hit. Their friends on the bank cheered and raised soft drinks to smiling lips.

I shook the ice in my glass and stood. Outside, wind drove snow against the trailer; the windows hummed, and the curtains quivered in cross-drafts. The kids in the commercial cannon- balled from overhanging rocks into the graceful slow motion of endless summer fun.

I turned off the set. The television was new, but reception this far out was seldom clear. A satellite dish would be the ticket, and I smiled to think of my folks' place—down in the Big Hole Valley—with just a radio.

At the breakfast counter I parted the curtains. Our Christmas tree rolled across the yard, bits of tinsel whipping in the frozen boughs. Snow had drifted to the third cinder block in the tractor shed wall, but it wasn't snow that got you up here, like in the Big Hole. It was wind. And even if this was still Montana, I felt like a stranger so far out in the open.

Cody had started the next day's bread at the sink, and her dark arms were dusted white to her rolled sleeves, her jeans already spotted with flour. It seemed unlikely, a woman who looked like that, baking bread in the kitchenette of a mobile home, and as I watched her, I felt again the mild shock of finding myself on leased dryland with her. The difference in our ages alone had been reason enough for doubt, but as time passed, I found that I was willing to believe.

"Twenty below riding a thirty-mile-an-hour wind," I said. "We should have sold the steers in October instead of waiting like the bank wanted." Snow sifted across the yard, rising like smoke through auras of mercury-vapor light above the feed lot.

"The bank is the boss, Pard." Cody folded the dough back on itself and looked at me. "Relax. It could be worse, old man." She blew strands of her black hair away from her face and shook her head. I reached over and brushed her hair back with the flat of my hand, then put two fingers in the flour on the counter and touched her cheek, leaving white dots on her mahogany skin. She ducked away from me with that look of hers and tried to rub the flour off with her shoulder. The smile lingered, though, as she reached up and smudged my nose. "You're a worrier is your problem," she said.

I slipped my arm around her and found her ribs with my fingers. "Worry about this," I whispered and felt her body fill with electric strength. I put my face in her hair and held her just off the floor until she began to relax. The last time we got going we broke a chair in the kitchen set.

After ten months we still played with each other, as proof, perhaps, that we'd be all right, that the distance to town and the fifteen years between us wouldn't matter. But in spite of the teasing, an early winter on a leased place seemed a hard way to start all over.

It might not have been the telephone but wind in the trailer skirts that woke me. The bedroom had gone cold, and it seemed we'd slept most of the night. I could hear Cody's voice down the hall in the spare bedroom we used as an office. The clock radio's luminous digits said 4:37.

I turned up the electric blanket, closed my eyes, and found myself standing in an irrigation ditch, shoveling mud onto a canvas dam and watching the metallic progress of water as it flooded my father's fields. Cottonwoods flanked the river, and in the trees, I could see the Percheron Norman teams we used for haying, lazing in tandem through the shade. The water in the ditch was so cold it cramped my legs.

" . . . up," Cody said. "Wake up, Clayton."

I shielded my eyes from the ceiling light with my arm and looked at Cody leaning over me. Her robe fell open, and I slipped my hand inside the terry cloth and let it ride the length of her back. At her thigh, I turned the robe aside to see the rose tattooed on the inside swale of her hip.

"Come have some coffee," she said, taking my hand and pulling me up. "I need to talk to you."

She pulled until I was sitting, then gathered her clothes and went off barefoot down the hallway toward the bathroom, walking hard on her heels. I put my arms on my knees and my head on my arms; I closed my eyes and tried to go back to the ditch. My right knee made a lump under my arm; a knee the size of a grapefruit. It always would be, the doctors said, and it ached if I didn't use the brace.

The smell of black soil soured by water lingered from the dream. It came to me at odd times, that odor of place and youth. The smell of home. My old man had married again at seventy-four. His bride owned the black mud now.

The Mr. Coffee was going when I got to the kitchen. Cody leaned against the counter, standing with one foot on the other as she smoked a Camel filter. She was wearing a pair of slippers that looked like mallards. Execuducks. I'd ordered them as a joke from an ad in one of Cody's magazines because she did our books. The slippers were for successful people who already had everything.

I pulled back the curtain at the sink. Pellets of snow struck the window like shot. I couldn't even see the diesel tank, twenty yards away. As I stepped back, I saw my reflection on the glass, my sleep-straightened hair standing as if in comic fright.

"Honey," Cody said. "That was TJ's mother on the phone. Are you awake?" She drew on her cigarette as if she needed it to breathe.

"I'm awake." I took two porcelain cafe cups from the drainboard and watched the coffee rise in the Pyrex pot. "TJ's got a mother?" I said.

Cody turned away to snub out the butt, and I looked at the clean lines of her back and legs, the currents of black hair spilling off her shoulders. In profile the blood really showed: Plains Cree and French, although her father, she thought, had been a Harp. I wondered how TJ Rountree, a person we did not often mention, had managed to get me out of bed.

With him it could be anything. I'd known him when he was just starting out on broncs, a skinny kid, who at first took a hell of a beating. But he toughened in his twenties, getting hard and limber as a bullprick whip. Over the years, I'd helped him off some winners, and for a while in the early '80s, it looked like he could be somebody. On his way down, he met Cody, and they ran together for a couple seasons, until I found her one night passed out in the grass behind the horse trailers at the Last Chance Stampede, lying there where Rountree left her. I got some help and took her to the hospital. After she took the cure, we started seeing each other. When we got married, we acted like Rountree had never been born.

"He's in Missoula," Cody said. She filled our cups and put cream on the table for hers. She lit another cigarette. "In the hospital."

The coffee was strong, although it would have been better the way I used to drink it, with half a shot to the cup. I couldn't do that anymore, living with Cody. I had two drinks a night and put the bottle away. Cody claimed that having whiskey around the house didn't bother her. When she'd been drinking, she went mostly with wine. Still, I kept the bottle out of sight. "He drying out or what?" I asked.

Cody nodded. "Bleeding shits, shakes, scared half crazy. His mom is there with him."

"Now it's Mom," I said. I sat down at the chrome and Formica table. Like the rest of the furniture, it had come with the trailer and had no connection to the past. "So what does Mom want from us?"

Cody stared at her slippers, cigarette smoke boiling from her nose. The one thing you notice right off about reformed drunks is the cigarettes and coffee. "He just waited too long," she said. "He thought he could cowboy up and go cold turkey. He was in some kind of shock by the time they got to him. He's asking for me."

"Well kiss my ass and call me Mildred," I said. "That takes guts." I started to stand, my knee popped, and I almost went down. But in that instant of vertigo before I caught the table, I understood something that had been there all along just under the surface. I saw why we'd never had a real fight, Cody and I. We called it love, but we knew we'd kill each other if we ever got started. As I looked at her I saw that we both understood it now.

"I've got to go," she said. "He's hurting and he's scared." She walked around the table and put her hand on my arm. I didn't know what to do, and I knew whatever I said would be wrong. I touched her hair. "I'll be needing the truck in the afternoons to feed," I said.

"Maybe the bus then," Cody answered. She slipped her arm under mine and hugged my waist. "If you'd just drive me in."

When it was light enough to see outside I started the truck, fed the horses and checked the stock tank heaters. The wind tapered off at dawn and morning broke clear, not a cloud from the Missouri to the Rocky Mountain Front. Smoke from the idling truck rose in vertical white contrails against a sea-blue sky. I thought about taking Cody to Great Falls for the bus, and I didn't believe, when it came right down to it, that we'd go. She would change her mind, or I'd say no, or, maybe Rountree would do the right thing for a change and die before we left.

Cody'd been through a bunch of men when she was running, but I could never understand why she'd ended up with him—a man so obviously out for himself. Winning a few in a row can turn your head, although when I'd been riding saddle broncs I hadn't lasted long enough to discover how I'd act on a roll. A chute post got my knee my second season, and riding pickup was about as close to winners as I got on the summer circuit.

We didn't have much to say during breakfast, and I tried for some restraint. It didn't work. Finally I said, "Okay. Tell me why."

She looked up, putting those black eyes on me. "Just don't," she said with a twist of her mouth. "Just don't you start."

"I need an answer," I told her and heard in the sound of my voice how much I meant it.

"Because," she said and took her dishes to the sink where she started to wash them, then one by one smashed each piece against the divider. She had to hit the cup three times before it broke, but when it did, chips cleared the drainboard and ricocheted off the microwave. When she finished, she took the porcelain handle from her fingers and put it on the table. She looked outside at the glare of sky on empty space. "Because he tried to love me," she said. "It wasn't easy for him, like it is for you, but he tried."

"And you drank yourself stupid, it was so good."

Cody turned her glistening eyes back to me. I'd never seen her cry, and she did not cry then; she stood at the sink, gazing at me, through cataracts of ice. "That's right," she said. "It was good. I just did not know how to face it sober."

I stood outside in the concrete forebay until the driver closed the luggage compartment doors and climbed aboard. Cody looked out the tinted window. Her face was green, her loose black hair clasped behind each ear by a beadwork barrette. A green Indian on her way to town. The driver ground gears and released the brakes, and Cody raised one hand. I shook my head and she looked away.

I went inside and walked around until I could feel my leg. The people waiting on the benches seemed to have been abandoned there in their winter clothes. Three bums sat together by the wall lockers, not going anywhere, just sitting quietly, sharing warmth, until someone threw them out. A woman from Rocky Boy or Harlem held a sleeping child—a grandson perhaps. Leaving the reservation or going back; she could have been Cody's mother, the child, mine.

Cody was in motion. As I walked to the truck I knew I had a choice: I could drive home and talk to the cows and wait, or I could move too. Momentum seemed the only answer.

Rising exhaust and river steam yellowed the frozen midday sky. Alone in the lanes of traffic, I felt somehow freed, opened to all the possibilities of so many people moving at such a pace. I drew five hundred dollars in cash at the branch bank on 10th Avenue South and drove on to the Holiday Village where I walked the mall looking in all the windows.

At the Westerners' I found a pin-stripe Fenton and a pair of gabardine slacks that matched. The fitting room was tight, but I managed to change without removing my brace. I topped off the shirt and pants with a black scarf and a pearl-gray Stetson. The clerk put my work clothes in a Westerners' sack. I felt dressed and ready; the sack suggested purchases in reserve.

I was surprised to see kids on every level, crowding the record stores, buying clothes, clowning on the escalators. Some of them wandered in pairs, holding hands. Some embraced in darker passageways near the theater, waiting for the matinee. Most seemed bored by the presence of so much merchandise.

Posters in the windows at Adventure Travel showed mossy castles in the Highlands, high-rise hotels in the Caribbean, an airliner in flight above white-domed clouds, and high-breasted girls in bikinis. I went inside and looked at more posters, at casinos in the desert, at tanned skin fronting white sand beaches, at coconut palms silhouetted against atomic skies. All the places I would never go.

When the travel agent came over, I pointed to an aerial shot of a beach at Mazatlan. "How much one way?" I asked.

She figured up a flight schedule by way of Denver and El Paso. "For one?" she asked without looking away from the terminal.

I told her yes and she touched more keys.

"One way, coach, is three hundred and sixty dollars—during our Winter Traveler's Special," she said.

"That's not that much, is it?"

She looked up. "My boyfriend and I went down last year. We stayed on the beach at Teacapan. We fell in love with it." She smiled. Her green eyes were bright as bottle glass in the glow of the screen.

I drove out to the Tropicana Club near the front gate of Malmstrom Air Force Base and went in to plan my future. The place was already in full swing, mostly airmen in civvies, a few wheat farmers in town for the day, a cowboy or two, and some poker machine apes—everyone drinking loud or watching two strobe-lit women who danced in wrought-iron cages swinging from the ceiling on chains. I walked to the end of the bar, as close to the cages as I could get, and put my Carhartt coat on a stool. The bartender gave me a napkin. I noticed a blender on the backbar. "Pina colada," I said. "Make it a pitcher."

The place could have been a warehouse: black cinder block walls with palm trees painted here and there in DayGlo greens, a tequila-sunset mural backing the bandstand. Music throbbed from the darkest corners. Overhead spots threw multicolored cones of light on the dancers. The closest girl took off her top, twirled it and rotated her small breasts in the opposite direction. The guy next to me squirmed and grinned. He was wearing a mesh cap that bore the winged Dekalb corn cob. "She really puts out," he said and turned back to love her.

She was oriental, Korean maybe. She looked into the colored lights and bopped away without seeming to notice the music. The other girl was very white, with dark red hair flounced into lazy curls. She seemed a little stiff, as if, perhaps, she was new to the cage.

The bartender put a fishbowl on my napkin and filled it with froth. "You want the umbrella?" he asked.

"Sure thing," I said and put a fifty on the bar. I rested my weight on my elbows and let the one leg hang.

He left the pitcher beside my glass and put a pink and blue bamboo umbrella, two candied cherries, and a lavender straw in my drink. He raised his eyebrows. "Just right," I told him, and he shook his head and smiled.

I was toying with the umbrella and thinking about Adventure Travel when it came to me: Green Indian. One of the illegals who irrigated for my father used to say that. Anything he didn't like or understand was an *Indio Verde*. Used to call my old man that behind his back, and son of a bitch, if he hadn't been right. I could see his face, the Mexican, but I had no idea what his name might have been. The old man called them all Manual, as in shovel.

I tried the drink and it was so cold it hurt my heart. It seemed almost perfect. All it needed was more fruit, more booze, and more light. I tried to imagine the perfect pina colada, freshly wrung from the jungle, to visualize the dancers' cages hanging from palm trees that fronted a white crescent beach with breakers coming in and sails like shark fins marking the horizon. One girl would be Polynesian, the other, old-country Irish. I was alone on the beach—the jungle at my back—dressed in a white terry cloth robe and Panama straw the color of cream, drinking the perfect pina colada and watching the waves churn to foam at my feet. In this state of mind, I owned the beach. I owned the dancers.

The music ended, the lights went down, and several airmen struggled to help the women from their pens. They got the job done, handing the dancers down like frozen beef. I closed my eyes. I wanted to stand centered between palms and watch the sea. I wanted it all: salt winds and sea warmth, sand burning the soles of my feet, the flash of endless ocean seared by sky.

I took out my wallet and flipped through my cards. Nothing on American Express or the Discover Card so far this month. The Visa looked good too. The MasterCard could stand another fifteen hundred, and there was my bank card, like an ace in the hole. I took them from their plastic pockets and spread them on the bar like a poker hand. I had some money tucked away at a bank in Butte. I could do it. I could be a wanderer in the world. I could go to the swimming hole every day.

I wondered if Cody was there yet, and how long it would take Rountree to cash in or straighten out once she found him. I wondered what she had hoped to accomplish beyond trying to do the right thing. I wondered what she would do if TJ cleaned up his act.

The dancers came along the bar, teasing the drinkers. The girl with red hair stopped to toy with my friend in the Dekalb cap. He was having fun now, all wiggly on his stool, making signs with his hands. She smiled with her teeth, a thirsty dust-bowl look of accommodation. She nodded at what he was saying, cut her eyes to me and noticed my drink. She looked down at my plastic full house and smiled again. Her outfit was mostly moccasins and strings of leather—some sort of vampy Mohawk motif. I took my Carhartt from the stool and held it out for her by the collar. She slipped into it like a cape, and the coat made her seem small. "Are those hot?" she asked, looking at the cards.

"Not yet," I answered.

She bent over the bar for a closer look then pulled the coat tight from inside, hiding her arms. "So?" she said.

"It has to do with green Indians," I said. "My wife took off this morning. I've got three hundred head of black cattle to feed for the bank and a trailer full of new appliances. If I don't get drunk and kill somebody, I might catch a flight to Mazatlan."

"I'm from Omaha," she said. "I know just how you feel."

"A couple weeks on the beach, drinking these beautiful drinks, and watching the water roll in."

"Yeah, right,", she said. "Like Jimmy Buffett there."

"Just exactly like Jimmy Buffett, frozen concoctions and all."

She took one arm from inside the coat and fanned the cards with the tips of her fingers. "Are you nice?" she asked.

"Oh, goodness yes, and quite wealthy, too."

"Come on. I mean, are you straight up or what?"

"Maybe if you're not so straight you don't lose so much," I said.

She shook her hair back with a quick movement of her head. "You won't go," she said. "You want it all back. I see guys like you every day, a handful of plastic and a plan. It's talk. It's a country song."

"Maybe you're right," I said, "but I'd lie to you for your love."

"You'll do more than that," she answered.

We laughed. She was on the road where I felt I should be, and the truth was I did feel better. I held out the fishbowl. "Here, kid, try some of this, and we'll see if you've got what it takes."

She raised the bowl like a giant shell to her lips and held my eyes as she drank. She closed her eyes, then drank again. When she handed it back she said, "My name is Danny. . . ." She picked up a card, tipping it to the bar lights, "Mr. Delaney."

"Clay," I said. "Mr. Delaney was my dad." I refilled the bowl, adjusted the umbrella. "One other thing."

"Right," she said and shook her hair back again. "I just knew there would be."

"I am going. I'm just not going alone."

Danny wiped the mustache away with the tip of her third finger and asked for the bowl again with her hands. "Of course you're not," she said.

At the Holiday Village, I put our tickets on my American Express and drew five thousand in cash from the bank. We drove across town in the blinding late light of afternoon with an accelerating sense of impending fun. From Airport Hill, where the sky cleared, Great Falls was lost beneath a sea of haze the color of sand.

The lady at the American Airlines counter tore our tickets and explained the flight changes at Denver and El Paso. She barely looked at the tickets as she talked, and it worried me that she might make an error. I could just see us boarding the morning flight from El Paso with hangovers, an attendant saying, "Excuse me, Sir, but there seems to be a mistake."

". . . luggage?" the airline lady asked.

"Just carry-on," I answered. "We're buying everything new."

Danny had an overnight case with her dancing costume and a tub of cocoa butter for the beach. Between us we didn't have a toothbrush. "I can't believe we're into this," she said on the escalator to the boarding level. She laughed and gave me her palms to slap. I laughed too and slid my hands over hers. We'd been laughing so much the last couple of hours my face had begun to hurt.

"Believe," I said. "Believe in the dream."

We had twenty minutes to kill. At the bank of international clocks in the concourse mezzanine, I told her I had to make a call.

"I'm thinking rum coladas," she said.

"Get some with all the goodies. I'll be right back."

I left her in the flight lounge and found a row of phones. I dumped some bar change on the phone tray and got the operator to ring McDonough's, our closest neighbors, three miles south. The youngest boy, Alfred, worked for me sometimes, when he could escape his old man.

Mrs. McDonough answered, and I asked for her son. When he came on, I said, "Something's come up, Al. Cody and I are going to be gone a while, and I need you to feed for me."

After a silence so long it seemed we'd been disconnected, he said, "Just a minute." Away from the receiver I heard him call: "Daaad." He sounded like a calf. Alfred, the slow son who would stay home.

"What's going on?" McDonough said in my ear.

"Like I told your boy, something has come up short notice, and I need him to feed for me. Cody and I are going to be away for a few days." I heard him breathing on the line. "So would it be all right? Can you spare him?"

"Are you drunk?" he said.

"No. I'm in Great Falls."

"Well, I don't know," he said, "what's going on with you people. That's your business. But I can tell you this: I picked up your wife at Bowman's Corner after she called here this afternoon. I went and got her and took her home drunk as seven hundred dollars. She ain't gone, she's out there with a case of Wild Berry."

"Hang on," I said.

"We get to your place, there's no tracks, no truck. She starts pulling her hair, for Christ's sake. You want my boy to walk into a jackpot like that?"

"You sure she's still there?'

"She's there. It's twelve miles to Augusta."

I felt myself sag. "Sorry about the trouble," I said.

"I've got more to do than ferry. . . ."

"Thanks again," I said and hung up.

I went to the wall of east-facing windows and looked out. I could see my one-ton in the lot, and off south, the slope-shouldered rise of the Little Belt Mountains—lit, like a memory of mountains, with alpenglow.

Above the escalators hung a mural of Lewis and Clark making their portage around the Great Falls of the Missouri. The men in the painting, all sinew and bone, strained to drag their pirogues up to the prairie. The sky behind them suggested midsummer and high adventure.

Danny was watching the American Airlines 737 join an accordioned tunnel outside. She'd killed both drinks. I leaned into the bar behind her and looked out through the floor-to-ceiling windows. I touched her hair.

"I've been all over," Danny said. "But every time I see my ship come in I get real goosey."

"Me too," I said. I paid for the drinks, and we walked into the mezzanine toward the boarding gates. Outside, the last direct rays of winter light stoked the Little Belts like bedded coals. She put her overnight bag on the conveyor at the security check. I emptied my pockets and took off my belt buckle. Danny went through, no problem. The machine went crazy on me. One of the uniformed women behind the counter raised her hand.

"My brace," I said and pulled up my pants leg for her to see.

Danny held the tray with my things, looking at the iron on my leg. The security lady came around the counter with a hand-held detector and ran it all over me. It liked the brace. "Okay," she said. "Sorry."

"It's all right," I said. "I'm not boarding anyway."

Danny fingered my buckle. When she looked at me it was with the dryness I'd first noticed at the bar. "Most guys just want to take you to Heaven at the Paradise Inn," she said. "But you, we get to go to the airport first."

I stuffed my pockets with change and put my buckle back on.

"You know something?" she said. "The last time I made it to the airport with a big spender like you, we went to Reno."

"How nice for you," I said and took her arm.

"What are you doing, man? I mean, I quit my job! I've got maybe three hundred dollars and no place to stay. It's January, Jack. Just let go, okay? I've had about enough for one shift."

I held her elbow until we got to Gate 4 where a line had formed at the podium for the flight to Denver. An attendant spoke into a red phone. He hung up and began taking tickets.

"Just great," she said. "Now we get to watch the nice people take off before you dump me here. This is getting creepy, you know?" She jerked her arm and I bore down. People leaving the plane glanced at us as they passed.

I took the packet of tickets from the cigar pocket in my coat and let go. I put some hundred dollar bills inside the folder. "I've got to go home," I said. "The beach is no place for a gimp. You go for both of us."

"Oh, come on!" she said, her palms out, warding off the tickets.

"And get a good Irish burn. And watch the water come in. And drink some real pina coladas."

The line ahead had shortened to three people. "Cash my ticket if you can. Stay as long as you want. Here," I handed her the folder.

"You don't need to rescue me," she said, her eyes beginning to shine. "Do you think I need you to leave town?"

"All you need is a white robe and a Panama straw and some shades. This isn't that complicated, and you'll make me feel good. Just go."

"Take a break," she said. "Give me a minute." She stepped into a ladies' room and I walked to a window and looked at the plane. My leg ached. I was beginning to feel the first waves of an afternoon hangover, and I realized that I was hungry. I drew a heart in the condensation on the glass and put a palm tree inside and shot an arrow through it. Cody would be passed out by now.

Danny took my arm. "Listen," she said. "What's going on?" Her hand was deeply freckled, and it was warm in the way of a warmth I needed most. In the hard light of the concourse she looked about my age.

"I called home," I told her. "My wife came back. She's a drinker and she's drinking again."

"If you hadn't called, would we have gone?"

"We would have surely gone."

"It would be sweet," she said, "the frozen concoctions and all." Then she took a hundred dollars from the envelope, handed me the rest of the money and tickets, and walked her dancer's walk back the way we'd come. At the security station she glanced toward me, shook her head, and kept going.

I waited until the engines gained pitch and the tunnel withdrew from the plane before I walked back to the bar, where I bought a pack of Camel Filters. I asked for a cup of coffee and smoked the first cigarette and watched the plane taxi north, its wing lights bright in the growing dusk. The cigarette made me dizzy.

I sat down and thought about having something to eat before I headed back out to the new place that except for Cody would never be home. I could not go home. But that meadowed valley with its beaverslide stackers and hayrake teams was always waiting in me. I could close my eyes and smell it; I could turn my head, and it was there.

I smoked another cigarette and drank my coffee and watched as the plane left the earth, leaping south into a winter sky that was turning with slow certainty toward spring.

CutBank Magazine 1993

Wings

Jeffrey waved from the shack and I eased my driver wheels onto the metal scale plate. When he waved again, I pulled the truck ahead to center the trailer wheels. I didn't get out of my truck and go in, like the other drivers, for my weight print-out. It was the pictures of wrecked logging trucks on the walls—especially Pa's—that stopped me.

Behind the little office where Jeffrey spent his days weighing trucks, a mountain of logs waited to be run through the screaming machinery in the mill. Every trip I took across those scales, I studied that log pile, and remembered the hundreds of nights I'd spent inside, running the head saw, saving wages to buy a truck. Looking back, the years at the mill seemed good. Sheila always had breakfast ready when I got home in the morning. When the weather was nice, we'd eat out on the back porch together and talk. She'd tell me about the correspondence course she had worked on that night, while I was at the mill; her face would light up when she explained something she'd just learned. And when she talked about maybe going to college, her eyes shined. She studied at night, so we could sleep together in the afternoons. I never understood much of what she told me about the courses that came in the mail; sometimes I didn't really listen, just sat watching her, enjoying the way she talked, smiling because she smiled.

"That's the last one, Buster," Jeff said, walking up with my scale slip. He took the cigar out of his mouth, handed up the weight print-out, and scratched his beer belly. "We're going to close her down, they say."

"The mill? Don't shit me."

"At the end of this shift," Jeff said.

154

I thought for a second. "I'll take 'em to Silver then."

Jeffrey's T-shirt had some holes in it; hair stuck out in little clumps, like dead moss. "They closed Silver yesterday, Buster. If you'd get yourself a CB, like everybody else, you'd know that."

I looked at the scale ticket. Four ton short of legal; six ton short of wages.

"Belgrade's still runnin' though," Jeff said, turning away to piss off the edge of the scale ramp.

"I got payments. I can't haul no hundred miles."

"Can't help you there, partner. We went broke again. Office boys all over the place with clipboards and white hard hats. They look serious."

"What you going to do?"

"Night watchman."

"Man."

"Listen, Buster," Jeff said, stepping up on the saddle tank under my truck door until he was level with me, "if I was you, I'd cash in that scale ticket there and any others you been holding onto for a rainy day." Jeff hadn't shaved in a week and his breath was sour. "This time maybe they really did go bust," he said. He stepped down, saw another truck pulling in behind me roiling dust and waved that driver onto the scale ramp.

Far back as I can remember, kids in town have been giving my ma, Martha, a bad time. The older ones mostly; little kids are scared of her. But they call her the Bird Woman and the Road Runner and such behind her back. They imitate the way she walks: the big purse gripped tight over her belly, her back too straight, the white ankle socks just a blur at the bottom of her skinny legs. And they copy the expressions that flit across her face. She walks around town for hours every day, looking for her little girl, my kid sister, Jane.

Climbing down from the Autocar, I saw Martha a block up the street, walking past the courthouse, smiling and nodding, talking to herself. Having her on the loose like that used to get me down. Folks in town think I'm simple too, but that's mostly because of my size. Nobody has come right out and pestered Martha in the open though, since Randy Jacobs started heckling her during the rodeo parade a couple years back, walking behind her with his arms folded back like wings, scratching at the ground with his boots, clucking and pecking like a chicken. I got nervous. Then I jerked Randy off his feet, and put him through that plate glass window in the Foodland. He didn't weigh much, almost nothing at all.

Martha used to get Sheila down too, acting like she does. Sheila helped keep Martha's place straightened up, and for a while she was the only person Martha would talk to, besides me. But sometimes Ma would call her Jane, and that scared my wife.

The bank was crowded. While I waited in line I dug the five mill checks I'd saved out of my wallet. Folded next to them was a worn, black-and-white picture—creased down the middle, corners wore away—of a little girl in a white dress, standing on the guardrail of the old bridge that spanned the Missouri before the Canyon Ferry Dam downstream was finished. Her dark hair is braided in little circles on each side of her head. A man's hand on one side of the picture steadies her.

Jane used to walk with her arms out away from her body, moving side-to-side with each step, like a little bird. And like in the picture, she was almost always smiling. The arm that holds her belonged to Pa. As far as I know, that is the only part of him, in any picture, left. Off in the distance, behind Jane, you can see a corner of the old homestead house where we had lived, beside the river.

I cashed my mill checks and made the two truck payments I was behind on.

One of the loan officers, Andy Little, who had been president of my high school class before I dropped out to work at the mill, walked over to me and asked, "How's the logging business going, Buster?" Then without waiting for an answer, he took me by the elbow and led me over to his cubicle, the way a man leads a draft horse into a stall.

"We're very concerned about the mill closure," Andy said, one hand smoothing down his mustache.

"Sure. It's bad."

"I've been checking through our accounts this afternoon and," he thumbed through some little cards with tiny square holes punched in them, "I noticed that your payments have fallen behind, the last few months."

"I just caught up on the truck," I said, wiping my nose on my sleeve. "The house payments are square."

Andy figured on a scratch pad for a minute. "Still behind $3,150, roughly, on the Caterpillar?"

"That sounds right."

"Do you think you can do it, keep up that is, with our facilities here closed?" He thumbed the stack of cards, then put his hand back to petting his mustache.

"You mean the mill? Yeah, I guess I can. Don't have much choice, do I?" My face was getting hot; Andy noticed, and put down the stack of little cards.

"Buster, we'll back you all we can, but there may be limits to what we can do," Andy said, smiling and waving at someone behind me.

Bill Lewis dumped a gallon pour-can of oil into the old Cummins while I filled the saddle tanks. I dusted off my name, painted on the truck doors in yellow letters that were supposed to look like fire: BUSTER KIMBELL, INDEPENDENT LOGGING. Red and green flames burned around the words.

"Guess you heard about the mill," Bill said.

"Right."

"What are you going to do?"

"Keep on cuttin' and square my tab here before I go broke too," I answered, taking out my checkbook.

"Ah, don't worry about it Buster," Bill said. "You buy a lot of fuel here."

"Yeah, but the way it sounds, I might not be buying it for long."

Bill looked up at me. "Might be closer to being right than you figure." He fished a can of Copenhagen out of his coveralls and dipped a chew. "Diesel shortage. The way things are runnin' now I won't get no fuel at all next week. "

"Are you sure?" I asked.

"Yeah," he said, following my checkbook with his eyes.

Inside the station, Bill rang up my fuel slips on his crank-handled adding machine.

"How about filling that tank at my place?"

"I don't know," Bill said, scratching his jaw.

"I've got to keep running to keep the bank off my back."

"All right," Bill said. "Tomorrow."

"That's five hundred gallons," I said.

"Buster, I'll do the best I can."

The wind picked up as the sky darkened with a little squall that blew in out of the northwest, carrying dust down from the Townsend Flat. Martha's laundry was scattered around in the yard behind her shack. When I pulled in, she was out on the porch, leaning into the wind.

I left her bag of groceries on the table, pumped her a bucket of water, and put some on the stove to heat for her dishes before I went back out on the porch to watch the dust blow by. The wind carried a couple of her pillowcases across a vacant lot and plastered them against a shed.

Martha nodded but didn't change her smile. Her blue eyes were bright in the iron grey hair that folded around her face and fell uncombed over the collar of her mackinaw.

"Listen to me, Ma. The mill closed today. I can't sell my logs there anymore."

Martha nodded in little jerks, her eyes nailing me.

"I'm broke Ma," I said, trying to get behind her smile. "Broke."

She saw that I was driving at something and switched expressions like changing channels. She started in like usual when something was wrong. "Nasty," she said, looking toward the river. "Muddy old water!" Her eyes went flat and hard as mirrors.

"Damn it Ma," I said. Then I caught myself, and walked around back to pick up her sheets and towels that were whipping in the wind, or stuck to tumbleweeds in the alley.

Before I left, I fixed her some supper and did her dishes. When I was ready to go I took her hands in mine, and said, "Ma, I'm going to stay on the mountain for a few days and cut. Don't get worried, and don't forget to eat. "

Martha brightened up, nodding her head, and pumping my hands up and down. "Jane's coming," she told me. "And we're going to pick apples across the river."

I unlocked the fuel tank for Bill, and got some tubes of machine grease from my tool shed. The Vespa scooter I'd bought for Jane, before she ran off to California, lay on its side, covered with truck parts and dust.

The house had faded a lighter blue from when Sheila and I painted it. I didn't stay here much anymore, but I kept up the payments. I opened the front door and looked around. The furniture and floors were dusty. Mouse tracks skittered along the baseboards. The shades were drawn; it was dim inside, like when I'd worked at the mill, when we'd slept seven years of afternoons.

Cobwebs swayed from the cedar posts on the over-sized bed I'd built for us; the room smelled of cedar, and so did Sheila's things, probably, that still hung in the closet, where I'd covered them with plastic.

A framed Polaroid snapshot, taken at her high school graduation, stood on the night table. Sheila grinned in her black robe with the gold honors lanyard around one shoulder. I stood with one arm down around her shoulders. The whole picture was a little out of focus. She had talked to me for years about going on to school, to college, but I knew about big towns. "What could I do there?" I'd asked her, and I told her no, until she didn't ask again and left. I looked around the room and wondered how she was; if she'd found what she had wanted at college; if she'd wear a robe like the one in the picture when she graduated again.

It was dark under those fir trees. A little spring flowed out of the rocks up near the head of the draw, where it got steep, damp, and cool smelling. The trickle of water splashed along clear and free for a few hundred yards, then disappeared back underground.

Working in there alone, in that dim, sun speckled light, knee deep in fern and moss and slash, I lost track of the days, of how far I was in debt, of where I was exactly. I'd remember Pa hand logging, and sometimes imagine he was there with me, running nimble down a log in his corks, his metal measuring tape flashing out behind him. And that little spring sparkled clear; so cold, the water burned when we drank it fast.

Each morning I shot a blue grouse or two while they were still roosted up, with the old .22 Special that had belonged to Pa. I soaked them in a mason jar of brine all day in the cold water of the spring, and had them for supper with spuds and ranch coffee.

To beat the afternoon heat, I cut from seven 'til noon, then fired up the Cat, bunked my logs, and dozed the slash into piles. Sometimes, lost in the snarl of my McCulloch 800, I'd feel like I was with Pa again, watching him and a partner fall a tree. Sometimes he'd sing out a line from a cowboy song, his big hands wrapped around the hardwood handle on the crosscut that whispered back and forth through the hidden insides of the tree, curling out long shavelings and sweet smelling sawdust.

"In the pines, in the pines, where the sun never shines," he sang, his upper arms bulging and the cords in his neck standing out stiff as choker cables. "And you shiver, when that cold wind blows." Then he'd wink at me and look at his partner, who was grunting and sweating on the other end of the crosscut, and Pa'd ask him if maybe he didn't want a saddle, so he'd be more comfortable riding his end of the saw.

When Pa was logging for Nieford White, he could pull that seven foot, two-man saw all day. He'd kneel, braced with one leg stretched out, and listen to the soft sound the cutting teeth made when he'd filed them just right. And Martha . . . Ma had been different then. She was good to us kids, always baking bread in the kitchen range, and joking around with Pa. Sometimes the four of us would walk the banks of the river in the evening. Jane could walk good by then, and she would laugh at the swallows and nighthawks swooping low over the silent waters.

I dozed back a bank on the uphill side of the road, and decked my logs where I could reach them with the leaky old Cherry Picker mounted behind the cab on the Autocar. The weather held clear and I managed to cut and snake out almost a load a day. Each evening I built a little fire somewhere near the spring, wrapped up the grouse in tin foil, and hid them and my taters in the coals. While I filed the six feet of Oregon chain on my saw, the birds baked a dry brown. Although the days were getting shorter, the evening light lasted longer in there beside the spring, let in by the trees I'd cut and cleared away.

Some nights were windy, like the weather might turn, but usually the evenings were still; only the sounds of pitch knots popping in the embers of the fire, the drag of my saw file, and the scolding of the magpies that kept track of my little camps. Each night I slept where I could find a flat spot near where I'd be cutting in the morning. Sometimes, late at night, I'd hear mule deer moving toward water in the brush.

One night I dreamed about the old place, where we'd lived beside the river when Jane and I were kids. It was early spring, the morning air heavy with smells of sagebrush, prairie grass, and river; gophers whistled on the edge of their holes; the foothills to the west, lit red by the rising sun. I followed along behind Pa, breaking up clods with my feet, as he turned over a new garden patch with an old horse and walking plow. The Missouri ran full to its banks nearby; mallards and teal, free of the land, winged close over the dark water. Pa hit something that stopped the plow. When I caught up, he was digging at a big head with broad, curved horns that was buried in the black ground. He scraped the dirt from the eye sockets and nose. "Buffalo," he told me, "maybe come along to drink at the river. Take 'm up and show your Ma."

I could see the old house—the one Ma's folks had built, where she had been born—and it looked the same: squared log, sided with warped shiplap and tarpaper, the grey plank porch leaning off slantwise. But when I tried to drag the skull, I couldn't move it. It held me to that spot like an anchor.

When I woke up, there was a light rain falling and my face was wet. I built a squaw fire and sat in the rain and tried to remember how it had been, living out there in that old house, before they flooded the valley with the dam. And I was surprised to see Ma, in the hissing embers of my fire, crying in the lamplight, Pa with his hand on her shoulder, telling her that moving to town wouldn't be so bad; that we had to leave, or somehow learn to live under water.

The Cherry Picker wouldn't lift any of the logs bigger than three feet at the butt. I had to build ramps out from the bank and push six or seven of the big ones onto the truck with the Cat, then top off the load with the Picker. I stacked them up until I saw the tires start to give, and spliced my chains to make the extra reach.

Sometimes I forget how good it feels to pull big logs on open road. The old 335 Cummins had four hundred thousand miles on the clock and needed new injectors bad. It knocked when it idled, and rattled all the way up to eighteen hundred. But going down the interstate on-ramp at Three Forks, I reached through the steering wheel with my left arm, skipped three gears, shifting both boxes together, and grinned as I watched the black smoke roll over the logs in my side mirror. I leaned back into the wore-out seat and drove, remembering Pa, jamming square-cut gears, smoking down switchbacks in the single-axle Mack that finally killed him.

That first load I pulled to Belgrade earned me more wages than a trip and a half back home. Rolling out of the mill, I kept glancing up at the check I'd clipped to the visor. In the distance, to the southeast, I could see the high-rise buildings at the university in Bozeman. Sheila was there somewhere. I thought about driving on in, and maybe calling her. But when I got to the interstate, I headed for home instead.

Trucks lined both sides of 287 the full length of Townsend. Some drivers stood talking, bunched up in front of the Husky station. A couple of them waved me over. One man, off by himself next to the highway, held a sign that said: ON STRIKE. They were strangers, men who drove over-the-road type rigs.

I was stove-up climbing down from my truck. A barrel-chested driver with a sunburned face leaned against the chromed bumper on a new Kenworth. He looked up at the torn crown of my straw hat. "How you doing, Tex?" he asked.

"Making wages, I guess," I answered.

"Is that right?" he said, just loud enough for all the other drivers to hear. "Well we sure ain't," he said, "cause we ain't got fuel."

I remembered my mill check. More drivers walked over, taking in my tin pants, braces, and boots.

"What you going to do about it?" I asked him.

He looked up at me, then turned and read my name on the truck door. When he was sure he had everybody's attention, he said, "Well, Buster, I'll tell you something. If we don't have fuel enough, in twenty-four hours, to get us home, we're going to plug up this highway tighter than a bull's ass in fly time."

I noticed Bill Lewis, standing in the open double doors of the Husky station, watching the drivers bunch up around me.

"Yeah. That's right!" another driver said. "We got to stick together. We got to stop everyone still running."

I played with some loose change in my pocket, and saw Martha breezing past the Dairy Bar down the street, talking up a storm to herself. I grinned.

Bill walked out of the station, wiping his hands on a shop rag.

"You think this is funny?" the man with the sign asked.

"No, Sir," I said, taking my hands out of my pockets. "Don't get me wrong,"

"Say Buster, could you put that motor on the stand for me?" Bill asked, pointing toward his shop. He looked around at the circle of faces. "It would save me going for a forklift."

"Sure," I said, and followed him to the open service door. Some of the drivers tagged along, talking among themselves.

It was Randy Jacob's 350. With all the plumbing taken off it didn't weigh much, not near what you'd think. I picked it up waist high, feeling the calluses on my fingers tear under the weight and carried it to the rebuild stand and held it there while Bill bolted it down. By the time we were done, the strikers had gone back across the highway, and sat shaded up on the loading dock at the grain elevator.

An old Pete rolled past, loaded with grain. The driver pulled air, waved, and kept right on going.

It was the last of the big timber, right at the head of the draw, where trees leaned uphill so bad I needed a dozen hardwood wedges to lift them plumb. I was driving a wedge into the back-cut when I saw them climbing toward me.

"One coming down!" I yelled.

The Forest Service kid and the deputy stopped, leaned into the hill, and got their wind.

I had saved this draw for last, this steep, north-facing gulch with its heavy stand of slow-growth fir. Some trees, like the one I was working, went more than eighty feet and had over four hundred rings at the butt. They were big and heavy as iron; the kind of timber that makes sawing worthwhile.

I set another wedge with the flat side of my Kelly and drove it deep. The tree moved with each blow, the top leaning over in quick little jerks, until she cracked in the undercut. With a squeal and a soft groan, she tipped slowly out into space, needles whistling as she gained momentum, until she landed sliding in a roar of breaking limbs.

"Buster, this is Charley Atkins," the Forest Service kid said, breathing hard from the climb. He watched us shake hands, then hiked off up the hill to see what I had left to cut.

"Morning," I said, looking at the big grips on his .357. Atkins was about my age, wiry, a broken nose. We'd been waving at each other on the road for a couple of years, since he transferred in from somewhere out of town. Still, we'd never talked before.

"Buster," he said, taking off his dark glasses, "it's your mother."

"Martha been snatching gew-gaws in the drugstore again?"

"No," he said, looking at the tree I'd just dropped. "She's in the hospital up in Helena. She got clipped by a car last night, walking the highway . . . out by the silos. "

"How bad she hurt?"

"Real bad," he said, hitching his belt to take the weight off his hips. "If you want, you can ride in with me."

"If it's all the same with you, I'll take the truck. I'll have my own outfit that way." Atkins put his glasses back on and looked over the old tree. "I don't think the driver was at fault. She was walking right on the road, dressed in dark clothes."

"Yeah," I said. "Probably so."

He looked up at me and said, "Buster, I know your mother isn't, well, right. But she was conscious last night when I got there. She kept talking about a little girl she'd lost. Do you know anything about that?"

"My sister. It don't matter now. That was a long time ago."

On the way to town, I stopped out in the middle of the Canyon Ferry Dam and tightened my chain binders. Water boiled out of the powerhouse below, churning the river white. Clouds rolled in over the cliffs above, and I felt the dam moving, like it was giving away, right out from under me

Martha's hair had been combed into a frosty tangle. Tubes and needles were taped to both her arms, and from the shape of the sheet, I could tell that some of her was in plaster. Clear plastic tubes ran to her nose. They'd taken out her teeth, and she looked awful old. I leaned against the rail along the side of the bed and watched her sleep, and I remembered how she was before the water came up . . . how her hair had been then, red and blazing in the morning light. I remembered her beside Dalstrom's old International truck, when they helped us move our stuff to town right after Pa got killed. And I remembered it was then, that Ma had started getting wild.

After a bit, I covered her hand with mine. A nurse came in, checking the feed-flow and drip from the bottles that hung above the bed. Two doctors looked through the doorway together. One nodded, and they left. I stood there—trying to keep out of the nurse's way, as she came in and out—until Martha opened her eyes. She ran her tongue around her dry lips and her eyes steadied on me. I could tell that she was full of dope, but I was sure she knew who I was.

"Ma," I said, and squeezed her hand.

Her eyes stayed on me and she started making a tired sing-song noise, kind of a little tune. With her hair brushed back, I could see how hollow her temples were; her lips, sunk in over her gums, were cracked by tiny wrinkles. She held me with her eyes, and I knew she was scared.

"Jane'll be coming home, Ma," I said.

She shook her head, slow, side-to-side, keeping her eyes locked on mine until closing them and drifting off.

It was almost morning, but I was still awake, when Ma woke up with a cry like a trapped bird. I stood up and took her hand again. "It's all right, Ma."

"Oh," she said, her eyes roaming around the ceiling.

"It's Buster, Ma."

"Home," I thought she said.

"That's right, Ma. We'll go home."

She made a noise like she was going to choke. I started to go for a nurse, but she gripped my hand. Her eyes settled on me and held me still.

Ma died before it got light, and she died without saying anything else.

Outside, in the pale morning sunshine, the old Autocar, huge and maroon, looked out of place, parked by the nice houses across the street from the hospital. The mossy logs, stacked up above the cab, didn't seem so big. And as I pulled the compression release and turned over the engine, Pa's song came back into my mind, tired now, and slow.

Trucks and cars and campers were backed up two miles from where the semis were jack-knifed across the narrow cement bridge north of town. I pulled off the side of the highway and locked up the truck. The morning sun burned off the chill. As I walked toward town, past the single lane of waiting rigs, I looked out across the backwater of the lake, trying to fix the exact spot where the old house had been, where it still was, buried under all that water.

Tractors and trailers were wedged so tight sideways around the bridge that I had to climb up and walk the concrete guardrail. On the town side of the bridge, highway patrolmen and striking drivers sat on wooden tables in the riverside picnic area, talking.

I walked along the guardrail with my arms out for balance. Below me, the Missouri moved in brown, dangerous eddies that made me dizzy. I stopped. I closed my eyes and listened to the water. I wanted that arm, the one that steadied little Jane in the snapshot I carried, to steady me too.

Two big wreckers started untangling the crossways trucks on the Townsend side of the bridge. People stood shaded up behind campers and trucks, waving newspapers for fans, watching, and talking among themselves. A lanky old man in bib overalls, his face and hands tanned dark as my rifle stock, stood on the side of a cattle truck, looking down into the beef packed in back. Rigs were parked behind him clear to town. He had a hot-shot and was prodding a downed animal, trying to get her on her feet before the other cattle stomped and smothered her to death. He looked down at me as I walked up and said, "If I lose any of these heifers over this foolishness, there's going to be hell to pay."

I climbed up the truck beside him, then went over the side and down into the press of cattle. I got the downed heifer by her tail, and managed to lift her enough that her hind quarters unfolded and she got her back legs under herself. Then I worked my way up to her head, got a handhold on the slack dewlap on each side of her brisket, and lifted her standing.

Working together, we got a lariat under her belly and made a couple passes back and forth through the slats in the Omaha bed, so she couldn't fold up again. One of the other heifers squared off and kicked the sideboards beside my knee with a crack like a .30-30.

Cars and trucks started to move both ways across the bridge. "Where you headed?" I asked.

"Avon," he said, wiping sweat from his eyes with a blue bandana. Somebody behind us blew a horn. "Thanks," he said. "Need a lift?"

"Just back up to my truck," I answered.

We rode along quiet for a ways, but when he saw my truck, he said, "Listen, you want a job?"

"Thanks," I told him, "I already got a job."

He pulled a business card from the chest pocket of his bibs and handed it to me. "Okay. You need one, you come see me. I can keep you busy."

I looked at the old man driving beside me, and at the card. "Maybe I will," I said.

The Autocar idled on the switchback below; the last four trees chained down on the log dolly as a makeshift trailer for the D-6. I was done, ready to pull out. I dug the cattle buyer's card from my jacket pocket.

In the snaky blue canyon below, a red-tailed hawk was getting hammered by some magpies. He couldn't circle much to climb, pinned in as he was by some steep limestone walls. One right after another, the magpies flew in and hit the hawk on his back, almost rolling him over. He flapped around, awkward-like, just trying to get away.

Clouds piled in over the Divide and covered the patchwork of fields in the Townsend Valley with scattered shadows. Flat and grey, the backwater from the dam shined like broken glass. I stepped onto the stump I'd been cutting when Atkins came about Ma. It bled little drops of pitch that stuck to the soles of my Wescos.

I read over the buyer's card. It said: ROBERT HAND ** Cattle and Horses ** Bought and Sold ** Helena, Montana. I tried to imagine hauling cattle for a while, sitting in on sales at Billings and Butte, Missoula and Bozeman, drinking coffee with the buyers.

The hawk pumped his wings, pulling himself up toward me. He let out a long scream, and the echoes bounced off the hills below. I thumbed the card and thought about maybe getting a new Stetson and some cowboy boots for nights in towns like Bozeman.

Across the valley, the Elkhorn Range parted a bank of fast moving clouds. Up there, on those rockslide ridges that had been too rough for the old-time hand loggers, new timber sales were open for bid. Maybe, I thought, I'd work over there for a while.

Out in the open and above me now, the hawk circled higher. The magpies kept after him, working hard to keep up, then one by one dropping back toward the canyon. I thought about nights in Bozeman, about the cafes and bars on the main drag, where I'd maybe see Sheila.

The red-tail rode the wind higher, circling up in that river of air that rolls rough-shod over the Belts, flowing down clear from Canada. He screamed again. I tore the old man's card in half and let the pieces blow away. Then the hawk changed his mind, folded his rust-colored wings, and slid sideways out of the sky, falling back toward the canyon like an iron wedge. Just before he hit the magpie, I saw him stretch out his legs and spread his talons. And I could see the black and white feathers, so clear, drifting on the wind, that I could almost count them.

The New Fiction Magazine (Great Britain) 1989

About the Author

Ralph Beer is the award-winning author of fiction and nonfiction books, including *The Blind Corral* and *In These Hills*. He has spent much of his life working as a rancher, sawyer, and road builder. Beer earned his MFA from the University of Montana and is a past editor of *CutBank* magazine.

www.ingramcontent.com/pod-product-compliance
Lightning Source LLC
Chambersburg PA
CBHW070918130626
46555CB00001B/191